KU-009-191

EVERYTHING'S AMAZING

(Sort of)

By
Liz Pichon

SCHOLASTIC

Scholastic Children's Books
An imprint of Scholastic Ltd

Text copyright © Liz Pichon, 2012
The right of Liz Pichon to be identified as the author of
this work has been asserted by her.

ISBN 978-93-5103-301-1

All rights reserved.
This book is sold subject to the condition that it shall not,
by way of trade or otherwise, be lent, hired out or otherwise
circulated in any form of binding or cover other than that
in which it is published. No part of this publication may be
reproduced, stored in a retrieval system, or transmitted in any
form or by any means (electronic, mechanical, photocopying,
recording or otherwise) without the prior written permission of
Scholastic India Pvt. Ltd., A-27, Ground Floor, Sigma Centre,
Infocity-1, Sector-34 Gurgaon 122001, (India)

Printed in India at MicroPrints India, New Delhi

First edition: May 2019
This edition: February 2020

This is a work of fiction. Names, characters, places, incidents
and dialogues are products of the author's imagination
or are used fictitiously. Any resemblance to actual
people, living or dead, events or locales is
entirely coincidental.

I'm in a VERY GOOD mood 🙂 TODAY for LOTS

of reasons...

read on

1. I've found **MORE** excellent ways to use Delia's sunglasses (that she doesn't know about).

Armpit scratcher

Smelly sock holder

Bird scarer

Foot Scratcher

2. I RAN **TWICE** round the garden before my toast **popped** up.

Which is a **NEW**

TOM GATES WORLD RECORD.

3. My TOAST DOODLES* looked AMAZING!

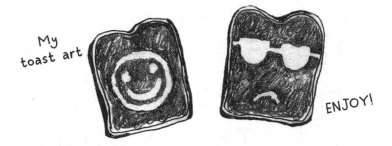

My toast art

ENJOY!

Especially the one of Delia.

AND I'm EVEN a 'bit'

EARLY for school.

—

*See page 407 for how I make TOAST DOODLES.

Mr Fullerman looks SHOCKed to see me in class on time.

He says,

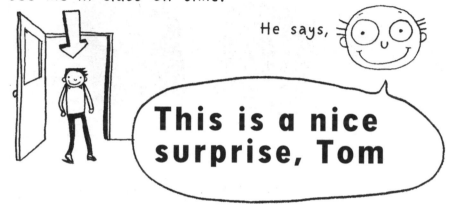

This is a nice surprise, Tom

and smiles.

(Which doesn't happen very often.)

Then Marcus pulls a face at me.

(Which does happen a lot.)

Nice

4

But **NOTHING**
can put me in a BAD
mood today!

Apart from these two words...

"Maths lesson."

Then it gets worse ...

"Maths lesson with Mrs Worthington."

... and worse...

"Now."

I've stopped smiling.

LUCKILY AMY PORTER →

sits next to me in class and she

LOVES maths. She can't

get enough of maths, which is handy for me

because THIS is how much I like maths:

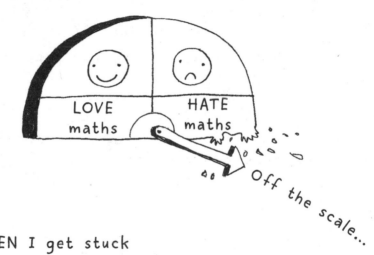

So WHEN I get stuck

on something tricky, I can take a

speedy look at AMY's correct ✓ answers

like this: ⊙ ⊙

But if I look the other way like this:

All I get is Marcus Meldrew's rubbish
answers. He's almost as bad at maths as me.
But from the way he *PUNCHES* the air
and says,

YES, MATHS, MY
FAVOURITE!

you'd think he was a maths Genius.

(He's not.)

Then Mrs WorthingTASH appears.
I call her that because she has a slightly

FURRY top lip. ➡

Just to be clear ... I NEVER EVER
say "Mrs WorthingTASH" out loud.
She announces to the WHOLE CLASS that if
we're REALLY good all lesson,
we can do her **SPECIAL MATHS QUIZ**.

"It will be SUCH fabulous fun with numbers,"
she says enthusiastically.

I doubt it.

Marcus tells AMY, "You can be on my team."

 Amy looks thrilled.

Marcus is behaving like a right TWIT. He keeps grinning and nodding at EVERYTHING Mrs WorthingTASH is saying. (Yes, yes.)

Ever since Marcus was caught CHEATING on the GOLDSTAR AWARD CHART, he's been trying to get back into ALL the teachers' good books.

It's sort of working, too, because

Mrs WorthingTASH congratulates Marcus on being

so wonderfully KEEN today.

He's sitting up STRAIGHT looking EVEN MORE pleased with himself now (if that's possible).

← smug

I tell AMY that "KEEN" is just another word for "IRRITATING".

Which makes her laugh.

Then Mrs WorthingTASH asks, "Would you like to share your joke with the whole class?" We both keep very quiet.

Unlike Marcus, who <u>won't</u> shut up. He's got his hand up and wants to know if we'll be doing TIMES-TABLE SQUARES today. Groan...

Then he says, "I've been practising a LOT, Mrs Worthington."

And Mrs WorthingTASH says...

"Well done for reminding me, Marcus. Yes, we <u>will</u> be doing times-table squares today.
Is everyone ready?"

Nice work, Marcus...

Still, it could be worse. At least I get to do a bit of drawing, even if it is just <u>lines</u> and numbers.

Here goes...

So far, so good.

12 this way ↓

1	2	3	4	5	6	7	8	9	10	11	12
2	4	6	8	10	12	14	16	18	20	22	24
3	6									30	
4	8									40	
5	10									50	
6	12									60	
7	14									70	
8	16									80	
9	18									90	
10	20	30	40	50	60	70	80	90	100	110	120
11	22									110	
12	24									120	

I'm busy trying to fill in my square (doing the ones I know first: two- and ten-times table).

Marcus keeps saying,

This is SO easy.

But I can see ◯ ◯ that he's made loads of mistakes already.   Ha! Ha!

I take a quick glance in **AMY'S** direction just to check I'm doing OK. (She's nearly FINISHED hers.)

Then it gets a bit tricky. I have to use my fingers to count on. (Doesn't everyone?)

Marcus starts DELIBERATELY counting **LOUDER** than me, which is really putting me off.

I keep losing my place.

TEN - FIFTEEN - TWENTY

TWO FOUR SIX

I'VE LOST MY PLACE AGAIN

He's driving me...

BONKERS!

I can't concentrate with him NEXT to me being all SMUG and NOISY.

SEVEN...
FOURTeen...
TWENTy-ONE.

I t's **impossible** to write my numbers proper~

So I start to **doodle** instead ...

and draw this.

Then I do another one ...

... and another.

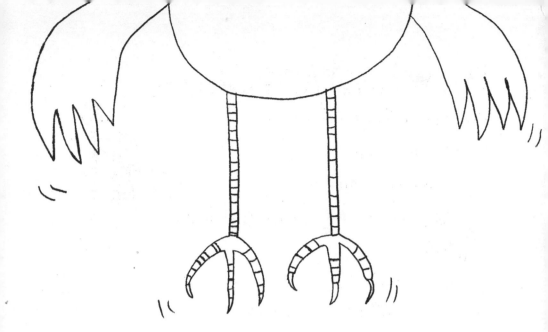

One more.

Mrs WorthingTASH spots 👓 Norman Watson *leaning* back in his chair.

She tells him to "*SIT UP PROPERLY*".

Then she says, "*Now, everyone, put down your pens and LISTEN carefully.*"

Which is a shame because I didn't get to finish this drawing ...

... OR my times-table square.

—What ogre?

Oh well, I'll fill it all in during the rest of the lesson.

I'm trying VERY hard to pay 'attention' to Mrs WorthingTASH.
She is busy teaching the lesson and saying things like:

Count how many dots there are.
Then TIMES that by the number of squares.
Blah blah blah...

Mysteriously my eyelids seem to be getting
heavier ⊖ ⊖ and **heavier** ⊖ ⊖
and **heavier.** ⊖ ⊖

I force them back OPEN (•) (•) by trying to CONCENTRATE on what she is saying.

The trouble is, it sounds like she's speaking another language (one I don't understand).

> Bloggle buggle wooble opple
> uggle Robble strobble bimple
> flung wallop
> poggle wobble flop loff.
> OK?

And to make things worse,

Mrs WorthingTASH keeps moving

CLOSER and CLOSER

to me so I can see 👁 👁 her moustache

a bit too clearly for my liking.

(It's even HARDER to concentrate now.)

I find myself (•) (•) STARING at the

number of hairs she has under her nose

and counting them. Which is helping me

keep my eyes OPEN.

I have counted almost fifteen hairs when

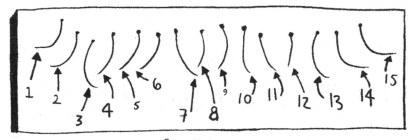

Mrs WorthingTASH asks me,

"Are you all right, Tom?"

I don't want to be rude or bring attention to the fact that I HAVEN'T finished my TIMES-TABLE SQUARE yet. So I am VERY polite and say...

"I'm FINE, thank you, MRS WORTHINGTASH."

And she says, "I'm sorry, Tom, what did you say?"
So I say it a BIT LOUDER.

"I'm FINE, thank you, MRS WORTHINGTASH."

(Did I just say that out loud?)

From the way **M**rs Worthington

is **GLARING** 👓 at me,

I'm guessing I did.

Yep ... I did.

This might take some explaining.

I try my best.

"Because I have a **TERRIBLE** cold, this **SNEEZE** just crept up on me unexpectedly when I said your name like this ...

... Mrs Worthingaaaa**TASHH**ooooooo!

 sniff
sniff."

I'm [not] sure Mrs WorthingTON is convinced.

Luckily for ME, Norman Watson comes to my rescue by falling backwards in his chair again.

Now he's waving his legs around in the air like an upturned turtle because he's stuck.

Mrs Worthington goes to help him and tells me:

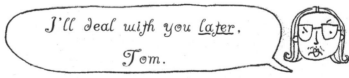

I'll deal with you *later*, Tom.

That doesn't sound good.

LATER

My maths teacher's name is:

MRS WORTHINGTON MRS WORTHINGTON
MRS WORTHINGTON MRS WORTHINGTASHTON
MRS WORTHINGTON MRS WORTHINGTON
MRS WORTHINGTON MRS WORTHINGTON
MRS WORTHINGTON MRS WORTHINGTASHTON MRS
WORTHINGTON MRS WORTHINGTON
MRS WORTHINGTON MRS WORTHINGTON
MRS WORTHINGTON MRS WORTHINGTON
MRS WORTHINGTON MRS WORTHINGTON MRS
WORTHINGTON MRS WORTHINGTON MRS
WORTHINGTON MRS WORTHINGTON
MRS WORTHINGTON MRS WORTHINGTON
MRS WORTHINGTON MRS WORTHINGTON MRS
WORTHINGTON MRS WORTHINGTON
MRS WORTHINGTON MRS WORTHINGTON
MRS WORTHINGTON MRS WORTHINGTON
MRS WORTHINGTON MRS WORTHINGTON
MRS WORTHINGTON MRS WORTHINGTON
MRS WORTHINGTON MRS WORTHINGTON

I won't make that
mistake again (out loud).

BrEAK TiMe

News travels *FAST* in our school.

Everyone seems to know about my
MOUSTACHE MISTAKE.

Derek is laughing a LOT

until I tell him about the lines I had to do

AND the EXTRA maths homework too.

Which he thinks is (harsh.

So 🙂 to cheer me up, Derek suggests we go and have a game of **CHAMP.**

It's an **EXCELLENT** idea.

CHAMP is a **TOP** game to play for lots of reasons:

1. You don't need much stuff — and chalk. BALL

2. It's super ={ᴊ} *FAST* ... so you never get bored.

3. Me and Derek are pretty good at CHAMP.

When we get to CHAMP CORNER some little kids have already drawn out a **CHAMP** square and are about to start playing.

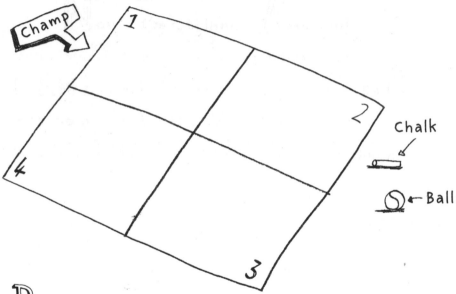

Derek asks if we can join in the game but they don't seem THAT keen.

"**I** promise we won't hit the ball **hard**," I say in case they're worried.

"**I** will, because **I** am CHAMP," the smallest girl says.

Derek whispers, "She won't be CHAMP for very long!"

Here are the rules of CHAMP in case you don't know ...

it's easy.

RULES of ChaMp

(It's a bit like cheap tennis.)

① **U**se your hand to hit the ball
(no scooping).

② **O**nly one bounce allowed but the ⬇ ball can go to any of the four squares.

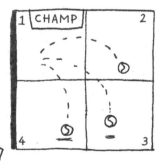

To BECOME the **CHAMP** you move around the squares. **B**ut if you're **OUT** you go to the back of the queue, _or_ to square **four** if there's no one waiting.

You must try to stay in CHAMP SQUARE for as long as possible to become the

(Oh yes!)

Our mate SOLID ‚ (who's the tallest boy in the school) wants to join in.

The little kids seem OK about it even though Solid looks like a

GIANT standing next to them.

like this

little
kids

When we start playing, those little kids are a **LOT** quicker than I expect.

I've only hit **ONE** ball when

POW I'm OUT already.

Bad luck, back of the queue for you,

the girl says.

Solid joins in next.

He's a bit slow hitting the ball ...

... but not as slow as Derek.

"You're out!" champ girl says.

Turns out that being as TALL as SOLID isn't much help reaching the low shots in CHAMP.

This puts me BACK in the game.

Missed

When Derek joins in, we try hitting the ball ...

... backwards

and ...

forwards to me ...

then to Derek

...to me

Derek ... it's the only way not to get out.

And works well, until I accidentally
pass the ball to the CHAMP girl.
THEN ... WHACK

39

The ball comes BACK SO FAST
I don't even see it go into

 the corner of my square.

"OUT AgAIN!"
the CHAMP GIRL shouts.

(This isn't as much fun as I thought it would be.)

The school bell rings, which saves me from more CHAMP humiliation.

"Let's have a rematch at lunch time?" the little girl suggests.

"Maybe not ... I'm very busy," I say.

"Don't worry," she adds. "Winning won't take long."
(EXACTLY.)
I'm *almost* looking forward to going back to class now ... until I remember what my next lesson is. (Groan)

ENGLISH

with Mr Fullerman

I {think} M**r** F**ullerman** has been chit-chatting with Mrs W**orthing**TON in the teachers' staff room during break.

He said what?

A**s** soon as I come into class, he says to me,

"I've been told to keep a SPECIAL EYE on you, Tom."

Which is a worry.

Mr Fullerman with his special eye.

Marcus has his book open already
and is busy drawing something that
he wants me to look  at.

What now?

Hilarious, Marcus.
You are the
funniest
boy in the WHOLE
school.

(Not.)

This is YOU, TOM.
Ha! Ha! Ha!

Just when I ⟨think⟩ that today's lesson is

going to be **WORSE** than MATHS,

Mr Fullerman announces that he would like

us to:

"Write a piece about a PET

or an animal.

Don't forget to include **LOTS** of interesting information, descriptions or stories, and FACTS about whatever creature you choose."

Which is

... and perfect timing.

Because last weekend Derek and I took

Rooster ⟨🐑⟩ ⟸ (Derek's dog) to the

local

DOG SHOW. So I have LOADS

of good stories to tell now!

But I can't start writing YET because...

1. J ulia Morton  is saying she doesn't have a pet and can't think what to write about.

2. M ark Clump has too many pets and wants to know if he can write about SNAKES AND LIZARDS?

3. N orman W atson has found a tiny spider and passes it to Julia so she has something to write about now.

Mr Fullerman tells Julia to

"STOP SCREAMING!"

and everyone else to

"SIT DOWN, CALM DOWN and think of an <u>imaginary</u> pet if you don't have one yourself."

(This imaginary pet might be fun to write about...)

I am a little tweet.

Better not.

R OSTER
at the DOG SHOW
By Tom Gates

I don't have a pet, unless you count
my sister Delia
(who's not really human).

mmm?

But my best mate Derek has a dog called

ROOSTER. He's quite small with long
ears and he eats a LOT of stuff he shouldn't.

Rooster is **NOT** normally the sort of dog you would enter into a **DOG SHOW**. **U**nless there

was a PRIZE for **DOG**

With the Weirdest Name.

He'd win that.

So when **D**erek and I saw ☉ ☉ a poster that said

ALL DOGS WELCOME, whatever shape or size!

We decided it might be **FUN** to take Rooster along. Derek said he knew exactly where the dog show was being held.

Which was just as well because Rooster had already chewed the whole poster up.

Back at Derek's house, Mrs Fingle (Derek's mum) suggested that Rooster might need a bit of a clean if we're taking him to a dog show?

It was a very good idea (especially after our walk)...

... but **NOT** easy to do.

Eventually we persuaded Rooster to stay still
long enough to get brushed.

There was a LOT of unusual
STUFF lurking in his **FUR.**

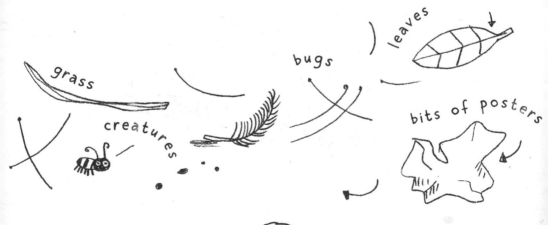

grass

creatures

bugs

leaves

bits of posters

After a lot of brushing, Rooster looked MUCH nicer.

But he still **SMELLED** the same.

"It's no good," Derek said, holding his nose.

"We'll have to give him a wash."

And that took even LONGER. We needed a few more doggie treats before Rooster

finally ...

... jumped into the dog bath ...

... and straight back out again.

At least he was a tiny bit cleaner.

Rooster **SHOOK**

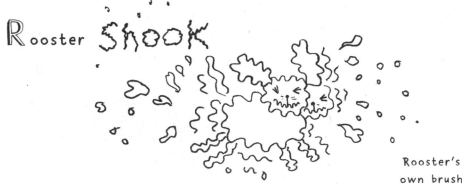

Rooster's own brush

himself dry, had a nice dinner and didn't
seem to mind having his teeth brushed.

Mrs Fingle thought Rooster looked like
a totally different dog. Derek said he
smelled different too.

I said, "It's called **CLEAN**."

"Let's hope he stays that way for the show
tomorrow," Derek said.
"Don't worry, he'll look **AMAZING**,"

I said.

Well, he WOULD have looked AMAZING. IF Mr Fingle (Derek's dad) hadn't forgotten all about the DOG SHOW and let Rooster out into the MUDDY garden in the pouring RAIN, first thing in the morning.

Derek PANICKED when he saw how messy Rooster was (again). By the time I came round to help, Derek had already dried Rooster off with two

56

great BIG 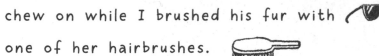 white towels.
(At least I think they were white;
it was hard to tell through all
the mud.) I gave Rooster a
pair of Delia's sunglasses to
chew on while I brushed his fur with
one of her hairbrushes.

Delia's brush worked a treat and helped
Rooster's fur look EXTRA soft and fluffy.
Derek thought it was unusual for Delia to be
so helpful. And I said she had NO IDEA how
helpful she was being. (Which was true.)

It was only when I stopped brushing Rooster
that I realized I might have
FLUFFED him up ...

... just a little bit too much?

"WHAT HAVE YOU DONE?

He looks like a poodle!" Derek said.

"It will flatten down by the time we get there," I said (hopefully).

"And the poster did say

ALL DOGS WELCOME,
whatever shape or size!"

Rooster was SO fluffy it took ages for
Derek to find his collar and put on his lead.
Then we had to *RUSH* to the park where the
DOG SHOW was about to start.

It was VERY windy and big

GUSTS kept catching Rooster's
fur from behind. Which wasn't
helping much.

"At least he's not the only dog who's all fluffy," Derek said, looking round the DOG SHOW. He was right, there were loads of dogs much SCRUFFIER and FLUFFIER than Rooster.

We paid Rooster's entrance fee and decided what categories we could put him in...

"Shame there's not a BEST FLUFFBALL IN SHOW," I said, which made Derek laugh.

We chose four in the end.

DOG SHOW

Name of dog	ROOSTER
Breed of dog	Who knows?
Name of owner	Derek Fingle

Category	Number	Entered
Dog With the Waggiest Tail	1	✗
Friendliest Dog	2	✗
Dog That Looks Most Like Its Owner	3	
Best Dog at Tricks	4	
Fastest Dog in Race	5	
Cutest Dog	6	✗
Best Dog in Show	7	
Dog and Spoon Race	8	✗

Derek handed in the form while I tried to de-fluff Rooster a little bit more.

Then I heard a voice behind me say, "Is that your dog, Tom?"

It was Marcus Meldrew with his tiny weeny little dog. (Groan.)

"No, it's Derek's dog, actually," I said.

Then Marcus started to LAUGH, and he said,

If there was a prize for the MOST STUPID-LOOKING DOG IN SHOW, you'd win THAT!

Dog

Rat

And I said,

If there was a prize for the DOG WHO LOOKS MOST LIKE A small RAT, you'd win THAT.

Which shut **M**arcus up.

Then his dog SUDDENLY got a

BIG WHIFF of BBQ and ran off in search of sausages, pulling Marcus behind him. Derek came back just in time to see Marcus being dragged away by his tiny dog. We were so busy laughing at Marcus running around, we nearly missed Rooster's first event!

Dog Winner

DOG WITH THE 'WAGGIEST' TAIL

was a close competition for all the dogs ...

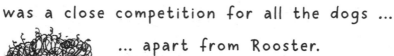

... apart from Rooster.

Who sat on his tail the whole time, which didn't help the judges much.

FIRST PRIZE for **FRIENDLIEST DOG** went to a **BIG** old soppy dog that looked like he was smiling.

DOG THAT MOST LOOKS LIKE ITS OWNER was next.

(Due to Derek's hair [not] being that FLUFFY we decided not to enter Rooster.)

Marcus was there and frowning a LOT, just like his dog. Who wasn't happy about leaving the BBQ. The judges awarded Marcus THIRD PRIZE.

So NOW it's official. Marcus Meldrew looks like his dog (who looks like a small grumpy RAT).

Rooster got a few (AWWWWs) AWWWWs

in CUTEST DOG IN SHOW
but nothing else.

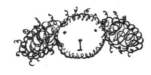

I told Derek there was always the
DOG AND SPOON RACE left.

Good luck! I said to them both ...
hopefully.

At the start line, the dogs were all barking
and sniffing.

Most of the dogs had entered and EVERYBODY
was trying not to drop their egg. When the
official starter SHOUTED,

"On your marks ... get set ... WOOF!
the dogs got really CONfused
and so did the owners.

It was **CHAOS!**

Rooster wasn't the only dog to run round in circles. Derek managed to untangle Rooster's lead and they set off in the right direction, followed closely by the other dogs. And that's when I noticed that MARCUS MELDREW was CHEATING.

Holding the egg down with his THUMB.

He walked really

FAST

right past Derek and Rooster.

Smiley dog wasn't far behind either.

I cheered ROOSTER! ROOSTER! ROOSTER!

Then Marcus accidentally SQUEEZED the

egg just a little bit too much until ...

 CRACK!

His thumb BROKE

the shell and egg went everywhere!

His tiny dog STOPPED suddenly ...

SNIFFED the ground ...

sniff

... then ran back to **EAT** the egg,
along with most of the other dogs too.
Who were all REALLY hungry.

Derek kept going and Rooster (who's not
keen on eggs) ran all the way to the finish
line, where they both crossed in

FIRST PLACE!

Smiley dog came second and a bundle of dogs
came third (at the same time).

HOORAY!
HOORAY!

Derek was VERY pleased they'd WON and so was I. He was presented with a FIRST PLACE certificate and Rooster was given a rosette to wear that said WINNER

DOG AND SPOON RACE
To Rooster
FIRST PRIZE

Well it DID say 'WINNER' until Rooster got hungry too.

And now it just says NER.

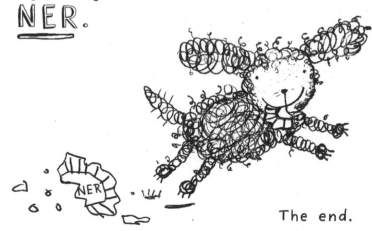

The end.

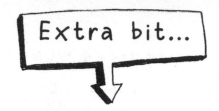

Extra bit...

Mr Fullerman, I HOPE you are <u>very</u> impressed that I have written a

TON of pages this lesson.

(It probably won't happen again for a long time because my hand feels like it's about to drop off.)

I worked VERY hard, in case you're giving out prizes or lots of merits?

Well done, Tom, you did work hard. Keep it up.

5 5 Merits

"You got **fifty-five** merits?"

Marcus has been snooping over my shoulder ...
as usual.

"Yes," I say.

 "It was a GREAT story."

(I added the extra <u>5</u> when he wasn't looking.)

He's telling <u>everyone</u> how I got fifty-five
{merits,} which is funny.

I keep a straight face ☺
     so he doesn't suspect a thing.

I've had **LOT**s of practice at keeping a straight face in tricky situations.

That was a close shave!

spill

straight face

Did you use my hairbrush on Rooster?

straight face

It's OK ... Rooster didn't catch anything from it.

Close up of Delia's brush.

When I get home from
school, Dad says he's got a  **SURPRISE**
for us [all] outside.

Mum looks shocked. (Really?)

I'm curious and Delia's just grumpy.
(What is it?)   (Who cares?)

He says,
"We're getting something **BIG** that

will make a **HUGE** difference to our (family life.)

76

Right away I'm thinking ...

MAssIvE TV
AT LAST!

Which is brilliant news, because our telly is very

 OLD.

But if I ever mention this to Dad,
he always says:

"**O**ur telly's not OLD. I grew up watching **BLACK** AND WHITE TV with NO remote control 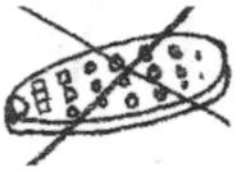 and an

AERIAL that you had to move around the room just to get a good

Picture

You don't know how lucky you are, Tom!"

Up a bit

Stay there

So I'm hoping TODAY
might be my

 day after all.

We all follow Dad outside...

It's <u>**not**</u> a TV.

Mum says,

"What have you done?"

Which is probably NOT the reaction Dad was
hoping for.

I quickly get over my initial disappointment
and decide that a brightly coloured van that
looks like a dinosaur might be FUN!

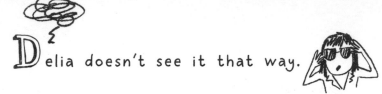

Delia doesn't see it that way.

"Why would you EVER think that

VAN was a good idea?" she asks.

"We can go camping in it too," Dad says.

"No. YOU can go camping in it,"
Mum says crossly.

Dad explains that he's doing some work for

DINO VILLAGE.

(Which is a really small 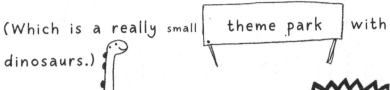 theme park with dinosaurs.)

He's allowed to use the van for  FREE as part of the job.

 Dad says, "It's not like I BOUGHT it."

Which is a relief to Mum.

Until he adds ... YET.

So while they are both having a **heated** discussion about (THAT VAN,) I go back  inside and take out the very important

BIRTHDAY LIST

that I've been working on.

I put it on the fridge where EVERYONE can see it (even Delia).

My list will remind Mum to tell other family members what I'm hoping for. ☺

I've had a few dodgy gifts in the past, especially from Granny Mavis and Granddad Bob (or **THE FOSSILS**, as I call them).

Love it
ANGEL

We called you that as a baby!

We heard you were very interested in trees

Everything you ever wanted to know about TREES

It's true, I am

I'm making sure that my list can be

EASILY SPOTTED ⊙ ⊙

by ➡ **THE FOSSILS** , who have just arrived to

"babysit" me while Mum and Dad go out for

dinner tonight. (They didn't trust Delia.)

 Granny says, "I'll have to get **BAKING**

for your birthday, won't I, Tom?"

I WANT to say,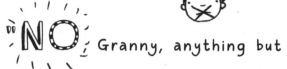

"NO, Granny, anything but

your COOKING!"

But instead I say, "You really <u>DON'T</u>

have to BAKE, Granny..."

But she insists that it's NO bother at all.

(Great.)

Then Granddad Bob picks up a couple of

spoons, puts them together and starts playing

them like an instrument.

 "I could be the party entertainer at your birthday, Tom ... what do you think?"

I think:

1. Granddad might need to learn a few more tunes first?

2. Granny offering to bake for me is a worry.

Granddad tries to teach me how to

play the spoons, but I can't get

them to **click** together like he can.

It's easy

CLICK
CLICK

Delia walks in and sees us.

"Doesn't anyone in this family do

ANYTHING

NORMAL?"

She's not very impressed with my

✱ ✱ ✱
BIRTHDAY LIST either.

Then Granny asks Delia how her

nice boyfriend Ed is.

Which makes her **s t o r m**

upstairs in a sulk.

 "Oh dear," Granny says when I
tell her. "They split up."

"She was too grumpy," I explain.

(I'm just guessing that's the reason.)

It could be:

rude,

miserable,

annoying,

sulky.

Take your pick.

Mum and Dad are late for dinner because Mum doesn't want to go in that van until it gets dark.

Granddad says they can borrow his mobility scooter.

"It's quite 'nippy', you know," he says.

But I think Dad wants to take the van for a drive. Derek has ⊙ ⊙ seen the van from his window and calls me up.

He thinks it's quite cool.

ring
ring.

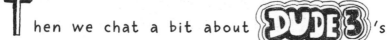 hen we chat a bit about 's

NEW ALBUM ⸬coming ⸬soon

(on my birthday list). And when we should have

our NEXT band practice for .

"This weekend."

"What snacks?"

"The usual ... caramel wafers, oh yes..."

 "Maybe that nice juice too?"

It's all **VERY** important STUFF.

T alking of  IMPORTANT stuff.

As I'm getting ready for bed, I notice that SOMEONE

(Delia ➜) has added a couple of

EXTRA things to my birthday list.

Ha! Ha! Very funny, Delia.

⭐ DUDE 3 NEW ALBUM

☆ Joke stuff

* GAMES (any kind)

Get me a Cardboard box
and fluffy earmuffs

(Spaces left for other ideas.)

(Close up of my list.)

MY BIRTHDAY LIST

☆ New guitar

☆ BIG TV for my r...

☆ Pet – dog/cat/rabb...

☆ Excellent clothes

☆ Cool arts stuff

☆ Treats – (caramel ...
sweets, MASSIVE ch...
bars, that kind of...

⭐ DUDE 3 NEW ALB...

☆ Joke stuff

* GAMES (any kind...

(Spaces left for other ideas.)

96

Then Granny says she's made me a **SPECIAL** bedtime snack. :)

"I'll bring it upstairs for you, Tom."

And I say "Great!" but inside I'm thinking "Oh no!"

Granny Mavis comes into my room holding a **VERY** nice cup of something that **LOOKS** like it could be

HOT CHOCOLATE with ORANGE FINGER BISCUITS!

which is ★**AMAZING.**★

Custard

Carrot

... but WRONG.

"Custard and carrot sticks, one of my favourites."

I think quickly and say,

"You have it, Granny, I'll be fine."

But that doesn't work.

"Brush your teeth after you've finished."

"Mmmmm, yum, I will."

I say goodnight and when she's gone, I hide the cup under my bed.

ART lesson

YEAH!

In the morning, Delia wakes me **UP** by **slamming** the bathroom door.

I forget all about the carrot and custard under my bed and manage to knock it **over** with my feet.

Which is not a great start to the day.

At least I have ART to look forward to this morning.

It's my FAVOURITE lesson. ☺

Derek and I are about to bike to school when he wants to take a closer look at the **DINO** VAN. "It's over there ... you can't miss it."

The van looks a **lot** `brighter` than I remember? We're not the only ones **staring** at it. ☉ ☉

$\mathbb{A}$t the school gates, Mr Keen is doing his usual greeting to everyone.

MORNING, MORNING, MORNING.

I tell $\mathbb{D}$erek it sounds like he's saying

MONEY, MONEY, MONEY.

I test out my theory by saying,

Money, Mr Keen really fast.

Mr Keen smiles and waves in our direction. I wonder what else I could pretend to say?

Derek thinks **MEERKAT**

sounds a bit like (Here, sir.)

"I'm going to try saying that at registration," he tells me.

I say, "Good luck with that one, Derek."

(He'll need it.)

In class, there are TWO words I would normally **NEVER** say together.

 **Happy** and **HOMEWORK**

But I can't believe Mr Fullerman has just handed out the **best** homework I've **EVER** had in my **LIFE**.

We have to decorate the covers of our

NEW sketchbooks **ANY** way we want to.

I can't **WAIT!**

I start doodling STRAIGHT AWAY...

But Mr Fullerman tells me to (STOP.
**"HOMEWORK is for you
to do AT HOME, Tom."**

(Shame.)

Mr Fullerman has set up what he calls a ⟨ **marvellous still life** ⟩ on every table. ⟶ 🪑 (I call it a plate of fruit.)

The class is split up into groups around each "marvellous still life".

He says we need to look ⊙ ⊙ carefully at each piece of fruit.

"Then use your pencils and paints to capture it."

(Like it's **ALIVE** or something.)

Don't move, apple

I'm trying to listen to Mr Fullerman
but **N**orman (who's on my table) is being
"**twitchy**". He thinks it's funny

to put a pineapple on his head and
do a **SiLLy** dance. Which
is quite funny.

Then Mark Clump says he can see
a REAL WORM inside the apple.

Julia Morton can't see **ANYTHING**
because **SOLID** is sitting in her way.
So Solid moves ...

and he **jogs** Leroy Lewis, who's holding a pot of paint. The paint goes **ALL over** the table and some flicks on to my book (that's a bit annoying).

Mr Fullerman uses his **"what do you think you're doing"** voice and a **STERN** STARE to keep everything under control.

He tells us to **"MOVE!"** while the mess gets cleared up (well, most of the mess).

Might as well put the splodges of ink to {good} use.

And draw this.

What blobs of paint?

Back to the still life now...

Title: Still Life (With Hand)

Norman keeps eating the grapes
so I draw in his hand (for evidence).

My still life is OK,

 for a first go.

Drawing the lemons

has given me an idea of something
else I could try. When Mr Fullerman's not
looking, I do a little

EXTRA still life picture.

Title: Mr Fullerman and Lemons

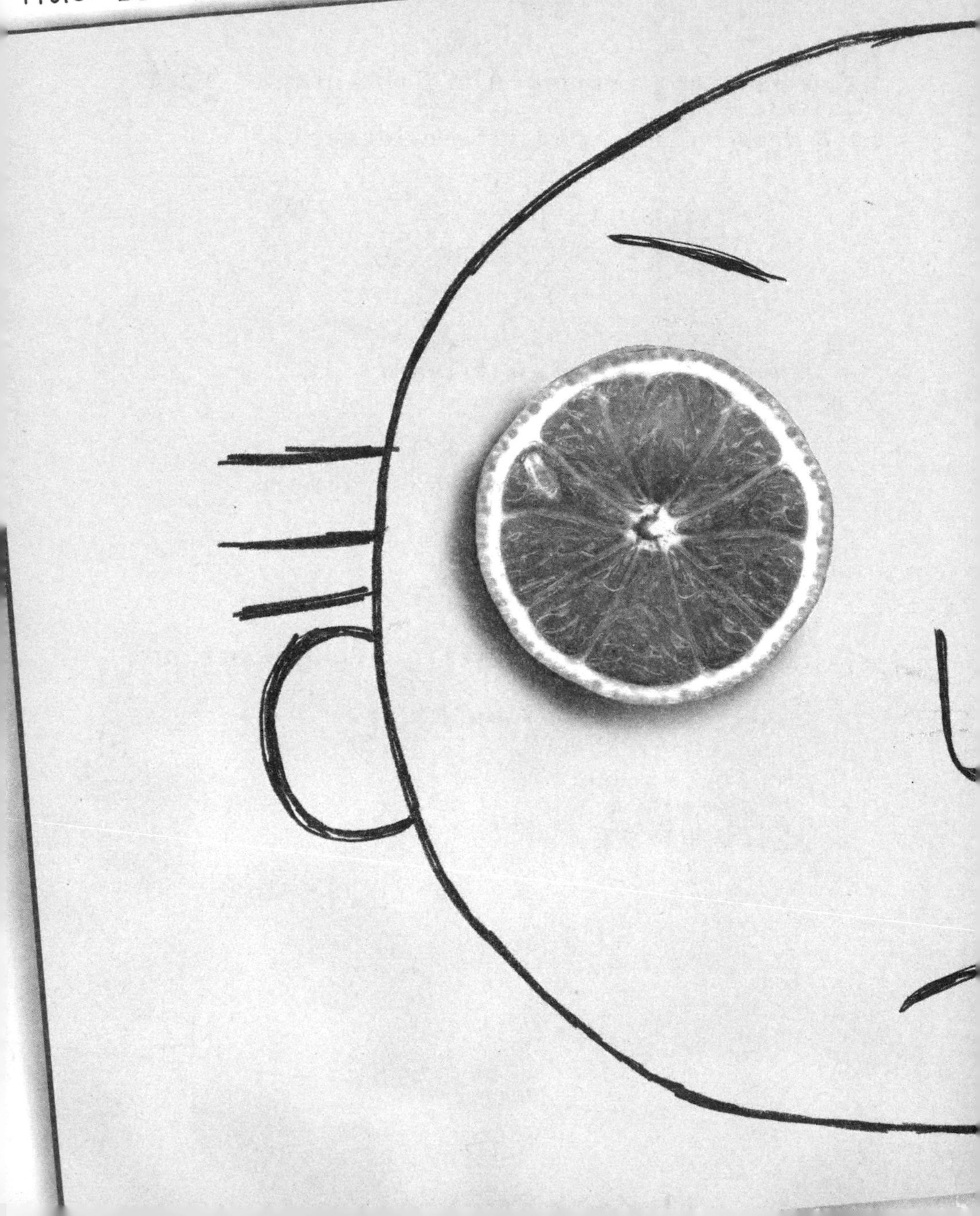

(No merits for me if he sees it!)

Amy Porter and everyone on my table are LAUGHING at my lemon picture a little too much.

Ha! Ha! Ha!

Mr Fullerman comes over and says,

"Less laughing, more drawing."

I cover up the drawing quickly.

Then I pretend I am studying the lemons CLOSELY before I start another drawing ...

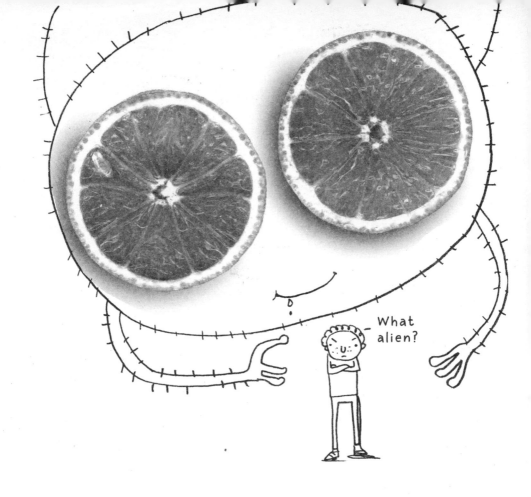

... like this...

$\mathbb{A}$t the end of the lesson,

Mr Fullerman hands out some *letters* for everyone to take home.

There is ONE WORKSHEET that we have to read ⊙ ⊙ at home, and also a letter about some sort of SPECIAL PEN and the latest **NEWSLETTER**.

The "PEN" letter looks interesting. I put that in my pocket so it doesn't get too scrunched.

The rest I am just about to STUFF into the bottom of my bag like **NORMAL** ...

... when **ONE LINE** on the **NEWSLETTER** catches my EYE. ⊙

OAKFIELD SCHOOL NEWSLETTER

ISSUE THREE

CONGRATULATIONS to **Claudia** for winning the POETRY competition with her "I LOVE MY DOG SID" poem.

WELL DONE! to Lucy in Class 3P for her sponsored silence.

Lucy stayed silent for a WHOLE school day and raised lots of money for charity. Which is fantastic.

Ben in Class 2D has PASSED his GRADE 2 violin. Well done, Ben!

And **congratulations** to Ava and Roman, both in Class 5W, who did very well in their tai kwon do competition.

GET YOUR TICKETS FOR THE OAKFIELD DISCO.

A SPECIAL SCHOOL BAND, **DOGZOMBIES**, WILL BE PLAYING AT THIS YEAR'S *SCHOOL DISCO!*

Please fill in the form and take it to the school office to get your tickets! They'll be plenty of delicious food and drinks available and your teachers will be showing you all a few FANCY dance moves.

IT SAYS...

DOGZOMBIES WILL BE PLAYING AT THIS YEAR'S *SCHOOL DISCO!*

Huh? That's news to me.

I ask **N**orman (who's **DOGZOMBIES**' new drummer) if he can remember **ANYTHING** about us playing at the SCHOOL DISCO?

And he says, "No, but I <u>can</u> remember what I had for breakfast, if that helps?"

 Not really, Norman.

Playing in front of **LOADS** of people at the SCHOOL DISCO could be a **DISASTER,** as **DOGZOMBIES** aren't that good yet. I tell Norman that the only way for us to avoid **TOTAL BAND** humiliation is to:

☆ 1. Practise more.

☆ 2. Practise more.

☆ 3. Practise more.

Rubbish

☆ 4. Or find a GOOD excuse NOT to play at the school *disco*.

Norman suggests we could always play

at the  again.

( first-ever gig).

"The crowd loved us! They went

Which is sort of true.

While we're discussing what

to do, Mr Fullerman only goes and tells

the **WHOLE** CLASS,

"This year at the school disco there's an EXTRA treat for us.

DOGZOMBIES, Tom, Norman and Derek's band, will be playing. Isn't that right, Tom?"

I nod (but not very much) like it's not a **BIG** deal.

Unlike Norman, who is standing up, taking a bow and pretending to play the drums.

Marcus says, "He's in your band? This should be a laugh."

Thanks for your support, Marcus.

When it's break time, I catch up with Derek and show him the **NEWSLETTER**.

I'm SURPRISED ⊙ ⊙

he thinks we should play.

"Mr Keen asked us to do it, remember?"

"No." 😐

"He was impressed we played at the old folks' home and wanted us to play for the whole school as well. For a TREAT!"

Not much of a treat, if you ask me.

Speaking of treats...

Mr Fullerman says that for HISTORY today he has a **"very interesting programme for us to watch."**

Which is excellent news because it means I can just sit back and relax.

Then do a few doodles while pretending to take notes.

The classroom is slightly dark, so even Mr Fullerman with his beady eyes can't see everything.

Which is just as well...

As it gives me a chance to close my eyes for a rest. Trouble is ... I keep thinking about WEIRD combinations of food I DON'T want Granny to make for my birthday.

Or **EVER**.

On the way home from school, Derek tells me,

"Playing in DOGZOMBIES

is fine, it's going to the SCHOOL Disco *
I'm REALLY not looking forward to."

"Why's that?"

Want to dance?

(I can think of a few good reasons not to go myself.)

Derek says, "If my dad volunteers to be

the school-disco DJ AGAIN,

it will be TOTAL humiliation for  **ME** ."

I'd forgotten about Derek's dad at the disco. He was ~~a bit~~ **VERY** embarrassing. Playing all his old records and a few new ones. He kept saying things like:

"This one's a classic, kids!"

And...

"CHOOON!"

into the microphone.

Derek wasn't happy at all.

He only cheered up when a teacher called Mr Sprocket SUDDENLY decided  to take to the dance floor and show us what he called

Old school break-dancing.

Look and learn, kids.

Everyone **CLAPPED** and SHOUTED,

"GO, SIR... GO, SIR... GO, SIR!"

Until **M**r Sprocket got a bit tangled up while spinning on the dance floor.

He needed an ambulance to take him to hospital.

I told Derek, "Now we know why it's called

 break dancing"

as we watched Mr Sprocket being driven away.

Derek's dad, or  DJ DAD as some kids were now calling him, had to pack up early because of Mr Sprocket's unfortunate injury.

Which was a **HUGE** relief to Derek.

(Shame over.)

Right [now] I'm trying to CONVINCE Derek that his dad might not even want to be a DJ again.

"Are you kidding? He's DESPERATE to get out his OLD records."

So I make a few suggestions:

1. We go back to Derek's house to make a plan.

2. Derek gets rid of the **NEWSLETTER** and any information about the school *disco*.

3. We eat some cake and bin → anything delicious we can find while thinking of places to hide his dad's records. (Bin? Under the table?) 😊 It's a good plan.

Back at Derek's house, between mouthfuls of

cake,  I do a good impression of Mr

Sprocket's BREAK DANCING.

Which makes Derek laugh.

Then Derek uses the cake stand

(now empty) and pretends it's a

record turntable.

"EMPTY!"

He says in a

really funny voice,

" This One's A CLASSIC,

KIDS. "

Followed by some of his dad's terrible **DJ** dancing moves.

It's **HILARIOUS.**

Then he says,
   "Guess who **THIS** is..."

CHOOOON!

Followed by...

"What's this ... another school disco?"
And I say, "That's AMAZING, Derek, you
sounded just like your dad then."

                         And Derek says...

"Hello, Dad."

 Because Mr Fingle is standing right behind me.

(Which is a bit AWKWARD.)

Derek tries to explain to his dad all the reasons WHY he REALLY doesn't want HIM to be the DJ at this year's school disco or ever again.

He says, "It was the most embarrassing day of my ENTIRE LIFE."

M_r Fingle is laughing when he says,

For **N**ow...

Then he asks **ME**,

"Was I *THAT* embarrassing, Tom?"

I [want] to say,

"YES, Mr Fingle. I was embarrassed
for you. Especially when you KEPT saying
'CHOON'; that was a total cringe."

But I don't want to make Derek feel any
worse, so instead I say,

"I'm just really glad that <u>MY</u> dad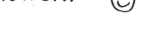
would NEVER be the school DJ,
Mr Fingle."

(Good answer.) ☺

And he says, "Don't be so sure,
Tom. I think YOUR dad has
volunteered to be the DJ this year."

"HUH?"

(I'm speechless.)

Mr Fingle is laughing and Derek is
rolling his 👁 👁 eyes, so I *think* he's joking.

I hope he is...

But it's EXACTLY the sort
of thing my dad would do.

(I really hope he hasn't volunteered.)

I volunteer!

When I get home, Dad's out so I can't ask him about being a **DJ.** Mum says she has

NO idea what he's up to.

"It sounds like something he might do."

That's just great.

Then Delia **BUTTS** in and she says,

"Dad's DEFINITELY going to be the **DJ** at your school disco."

And I say, "How do you know?'

 "Because he told me, stupid.
AND I've seen his special costume."

"WHAT special costume?"

"The one he's bought to wear at YOUR school disco."

Mum says, "Delia's *joking* ... I think."

She's not sure either. Ever since Dad turned up with the **SURPRISE DINO** VAN, who knows what he'll do next? Mum says she'll ask him about it later. But I can't wait THAT long. So before I go to bed, I take a sneaky peek upstairs to see if I can find evidence of ANY EMBARRASSING costumes that might be lurking around.

... It's **SO** much worse

than I thought.

In the morning I'm VERY tired because last night I had a **TERRIBLE** dream that Dad WAS the DJ at the school *disco*. He wore a really EMBARRASSING costume. All the kids gathered round ME, pointing and asking,

Dad?

"Is that your dad in the STUPID costume?"
"Is that your dad in the STUPID costume?"
When I woke up I realized that my dream could actually come true (which is a nightmare!).

AND to make it worse, I haven't forgotten about **DOGZOMBIES** playing at the disco, in front of everyone.

Now I'm late for school because the only jumper I can find is hanging on the washing line outside ...

and it's **damp**.

Dad suggests I "throw it in the tumble dryer on **FULL POWER** for a bit".

W hich seems like a good idea and works
a treat, drying my jumper
out nicely.

I'm just about to ask Dad about
being a DJ and [what] the STUPID costume
is for, when Mum RUSHES in and shouts,

"W hat are you still doing here?
HURRY UP ... you're
LATE AGAIN!"

It makes Dad JUMP out of his
seat and dash to the shed.

"I meant you, Tom. Go on, get going,"
Mum says.

I'll have to ask Dad later. Groan. 😖

I only *just* make it to school on time and run into class.

Mr Fullerman is ALREADY STARING at me.

He says, **"TOM, where is your school jumper?"**

(Round my waist and still nice and warm from the tumble dryer.)

I try to put it on and *that's* when I realize that there might be a very small problem.

My jumper seems to have ...

... shrunk

Quite a lot.

Mr Fullerman is watching me squeeze the jumper over my head. The class start

LAUGHING so he tells me

to **hurry up.**

I'm trying to stretch my jumper a little more by pulling at the sleeves.

But they won't go down any further.

Marcus is sniggering at me, which is not very helpful.

Ha!
Ha!

So I ask him,

"What's so funny, haven't you

heard of a SHRINK **KNIT?**"

(Good thinking.)

He says, "**Yeah**, right."

And I say,

"All the **cool** kids are

wearing them ... like me."

That's got him thinking.

I'm very convincing.

I still can't believe my jumper's shrunk SO much
in such a short space of time.

I wriggle around to **EASE** my jumper
down just a tiny bit more before
we have to go to assembly.

ASSEMBLY

Mr Keen, our headmaster, says,

"Good morning, Oakfield School."

"Good morning, Mr Keen."

Then he starts talking about **"this"** and **"that"**. I'm TRYING to listen but it's difficult to concentrate because my jumper is SO SNUG. I'm getting

HOT and slightly uncomfortable.

I keep moving around but it won't loosen up.

Fidget fidget

Mr Keen stops talking and looks

in MY direction.

"Whoever has ants in their pants, can they  **fidgeting!"**

(That will be me, then.)

ants

When everyone stands up to Sing
"Oh what a BEAUTIFUL morning..."

I take the opportunity to p u L L down my
jumper without bringing too much attention
to myself again. It's not working that well, as
some kids are staring at me.

So I pretend my tiny jumper is perfectly fine and STYLISH and definitely NOT a MISTAKE.

Mr Keen announces that before we all go back to class, **"Ryan and Kevin from Class 4A have a SPECIAL PEN DEMONSTRATION to show us."**

Then Ryan comes up to the front with his mini scooter. He scoots across the floor and props his scooter up against the table.

Kevin wanders along ... and pretends to find Ryan's scooter. (He's doing some **VERY BAD** acting now.)

Ryan shouts, "Hey, that's my scooter!"

And Kevin says, "No, it's MINE."

Then Ryan looks at all of us and says in a
REALLY **WOODEN** voice,

"I will prove it's **MY** scooter."

Then Kevin says,

"This **scooter** is mine,

SUCKER."

(Which gets a laugh because I don't think he
was supposed to say "sucker".)

Ryan says, "We'll see" and gets out
a torch.

He looks under the scooter and says, "Look,
nothing there..."

Everyone is leaning forward to see.

Then he [torch] SHINES his

SPECIAL TORCH and some glowing

letters appear.

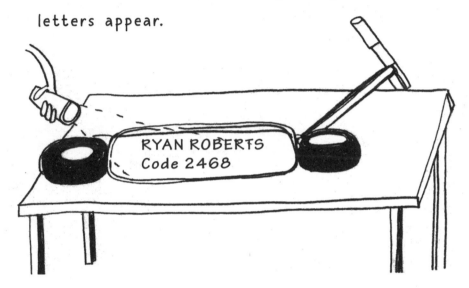

RYAN ROBERTS
Code 2468

"NOW there is..."

We go "OOOOOOOOOOOHH" like it's
a magic trick, and everyone claps.

Mr Keen thanks Ryan and Kevin, who take a bow. (They are looking very pleased with themselves.)

He tells us that CARETAKER Stan  has suggested **ALL BIKES** and **SCOOTERS** brought in to school should be marked with these

"ULTRAVIOLET PENS".

I'm thinking that this pen would be perfect to use on all MY copies of **ROCK WEEKLY.**

I t might STOP Delia
from pinching them and claiming they're hers.

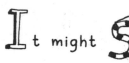
Mine

The possibilities for this pen are endless.

Delia's
boots

Delia's
a fool

Mr Keen says Mrs Mumble will be
selling the pens from tomorrow but we need
to remember our signed letters and money.

(I won't forget.)

Then he says,

"Put your hand up if you think you might like to get one."

LOTS of hands SHOOT UP

REALLY F A S T.

Due to my very tight jumper sleeve, my hand takes a bit longer to stretch.

But I get there in the end.

I see Derek at break time and he says, "What's with the small jumper?"

I explain what happened and how I'm trying to stretch the jumper out a bit more. Then he suggests a game of CHAMP might help.

"It's OK, the CHAMP girl is away," he adds.

"Maybe tomorrow."

Because I can't even scratch my head, let alone hit a ball. I spend the rest of the day trying not to move very much in lessons.

And explaining to everyone who asks that I'm wearing a very special SHRINK KNIT. (A lot of people want to know.)

"They'll be everywhere soon, trust me," I keep saying.

Home time and the end of the day can't come soon enough.

159

BIRTHDAY COUNTDOWN

At home, I have another struggle with my small jumper. Once it's off I go downstairs to search for a well-deserved treat in the kitchen when Mum asks me if I'd like a **party** this year for my birthday.

Normally I'd LOVE a party because:

lots of people = lots of presents

But right now I'm not so sure.

"What's wrong, Tom? I've only asked if you want a **PARTY**, not a plate of **SLUGS**,"

Mum says.

I take a deep breath and explain that:

1. Granny **M**avis wants to **BAKE** for my birthday. Which *could* be a problem.

   ← sausage on a cake

2. Granddad is a bit too keen on playing the spoons as my party entertainment. His false teeth will probably make an appearance too. (Which is quite entertaining, but not for everyone.)

3. I'm REALLY worried Dad has volunteered to be the **DJ** at my school disco. (And at my party too, if I have one.)

4. **AND** in case I'm not embarrassed enough, he'll probably WEAR that stupid costume I found.

I can hear Dad laughing in the background. He's been standing there listening.

(Great.)

"Don't panic, Tom, Mr Fingle was only joking. I'm NOT the school DJ this year and the costume is for something else completely."

Which is a  RELIEF.

 Phew

But Mum and Dad both say there's absolutely nothing they can do about Granny and Granddad.

"They dance to their own tune," Dad tells me.

Which is true, I've seen them.

I change my mind and tell Mum that I would like a * **PARTY** after all.

Then Dad says he has another **SURPISE** just for me... (Not like this one, I hope!)

He shows me some invitations. "How would you like to have a **DINO** Village **PARTY** for you and four friends, plus your two cousins? I can't fit any more than that in the van."

It's an **excellent** idea.

To be honest I'm SO RELIEVED Dad's ~~not~~ the school disco DJ I would have been happy with any kind of party surprise (well, nearly anything).

Happy birthday, idiot

Happy Birthday
TOM

I can invite:

 Me (obviously)

 Derek

 Norman

 Solid

 Mark Clump

 Cousin

 Cousin

Delia comes in and says to Dad,
"He's not having a party <u>here</u>, is he?"

Dad says "No" but reminds Delia
that I'm still allowed parties in
the house ...
"unlike you, after last time".

Good point, Dad. I wish I'd thought of
that myself.

Mum says Delia is very welcome to
come to my **DINO** Village PARTY.

(She is? I don't think so.)

Delia says,

"Let me think about it for a while..."

 "...Mmmmmm,

 no."

Which is another huge relief.

Now my party is all decided, Mum gives me some invitations to fill out.

They look a bit boring. So I do a few doodles, which I think is a **BIG** improvement.

My doodles remind me I still

have the letter about the special ✏ pen in
my pocket. I ask Mum to sign it and
😊 (Please) can I have the money too?"

(I'm hoping she won't give me the *exact*
amount, so I can buy snacks with any
change.) 😊 (yes!)

Mum wants to know if there are any other
important letters for her to see. 👧

(Just the school **NEWSLETTER**, and my
worksheet ... nothing important.) So I say, "No,
not really." 😊

NEW CRAZe *(sort of)*

There's only a few days to go until my birthday now. I'm officially excited!

(Must remember to bring my party invitations with me to give out.)

I'm forced to wear my small jumper AGAIN because I have no idea where my other one's gone.

At least now the arms have stretched, it's a bit more comfy.

Delia sees me and says, "What's wrong with your jumper?"

"Nothing, I've just gr**own**."

"Grown more stupid,
if that's possible.
You look ridiculous."

And I say, "Says the girl who wears sunglasses all the time."

Which makes her walk off in a

huff.

Derek has put a message up in his window that reminds me to bring money for the **ULTRAVIOLET** pens.

I have to remember to take my bike as well as my party invitations.
Derek is waiting for me by the gate so I give him his invite straight away.

He says, "Shame I can't come, I'm busy that day." 😟

Quickly followed by,

ONLY JOKING!

Very funny, Derek.

Now he's doing an impression of me looking shocked.

"That's not me."

"It is!"

I change the subject and remind Derek about **DOGZOMBIES** playing at the school disco and how we need **LOADS** more practice. "I'll ask Norman if he's free tonight when I give him the party invitation."

Good thinking.

When we get to school, I hand out Solid's invite but Norman's not here.

Solid says he twisted his knee.

"He was playing CHAMP against those little kids. They were a bit too good for him. Norman kept falling over."

Uh oh!

Which doesn't sound good.

Mark Clump is VERY happy
to get his invitation.

"DINO VILLAGE is full of
creatures and good stuff to do."

Which is

EXCELLENT

news.

But Mr Fullerman doesn't look too
happy. He wants to know if I'd like to borrow
a larger school jumper from the SPARE CLOTHES
box?

Errr, no thanks.

I assure him that my jumper is fine (now) and I'm planning to get a new one soon, which is true.

I hope I don't get into trouble as it is uniform, after all (just a bit small).

Marcus Meldrew is busy eyeballing the invitations on my desk.

He says, "What are they?"

I say, "Nothing," then he says,
"Are they your party invitations to
DINO Village?"

Marcus has obviously been snooping around again.
So I say, "Might be,"
and he says, "That's embarrassing for you."
"**W**hy's that, Marcus?"

"Dinosaur parties are for little kids,
aren't they?"

Then Amy sits down on the other side
and she says,

"Sounds like fun to me." Marcus adds, "Well, you wouldn't catch me having a party somewhere like that. Too BORING. DuLLO Village, more like..."

So I say, "Yes, you're right, Marcus, it will be boring and DULL. So it's just as well you're not coming, then."

Which shuts him up.

Then Amy says, "Am I invited?"

Which is a surprise. I didn't even think of
asking Amy.

Dad said I could only invite **four** people.
But I HEAR myself saying,

     "Of course you can come."

(I'll give her Norman's invitation.)

 Then she says,

    "Can Florence come too?"

And I say, **"YES**, I have her invitation at home."

(I can't invite just one cousin. So that's both
of them off my birthday list, then...)

Amy says she is really looking forward to seeing **DOGZOMBIES** play at the school disco.

And I say, "You are?"
and Marcus mutters, "I'm not."

So I ignore him and listen to Amy, who tells me that she's heard quite a few kids are talking about:

- **DOGZOMBIES** playing at the school disco.

- The new craze for SHRINK KNIT jumpers (like mine).

I'm getting used to people staring at my jumper.

small jumper

But I'm wondering how the other kids would know about **DOGZOMBIES**?

So I point out that...

"**DOGZOMBIES** have only ever played one gig."
(I don't say where.)

Amy says, "They must have read it in the **NEWSLETTER**, remember?"

(It's all coming back to me now.)

Not reading 👀 my worksheet before stuffing it into my bag turns out to be a bit of a problem, too.

Mr Fullerman has just handed out
WORKSHEET TWO.

(**WORKSHEET ONE** is still scrunched up in my bag.)

While Mr Fullerman is at the back of the class, I have a quick root around to see if I can find it. That's when I discover that due to a leaking drinks carton, they have both turned to

MUSH.

Never mind, it will be fine.
I can do without them.

Then Mr Fullerman says,

**"You should ALL have read
WORKSHEET ONE for your homework."**

(Er, no...)

**"Because ALL the answers for
WORKSHEET TWO are on
WORKSHEET ONE."**

(Uh-oh...)

Trevor Peters puts up his hand and says, "I've lost my worksheet, sir."

(This could be a GOOD time to mention my MUSHY worksheet?)

Mr Fullerman says,

"NOT AGAIN, Trevor?"

He doesn't sound pleased.

"Just share a worksheet for now. Stay after class and I'll give you a new one. That goes for everyone."

I keep quiet because I want to go

STRAIGHT to the office

after school and get my **ULTRAVIOLET** pen, NOT hang around in class waiting for  worksheets.

I glance over at Marcus to see if I can share his.

No chance.

He's got his arm covering his work.

Amy doesn't need her worksheet because she's memorized everything.

So I'm a bit stuck.

Oh well, I'll just have to fill in the _ _ _ _ _ _ _ _ _ _ blank spaces on **WORKSHEET TWO** using ... my imagination.

How hard can it be?

WORKSHEET TWO
Class 5F
Read **WORKSHEET ONE AND TWO** carefully, then answer the questions below by filling in the spaces.

John was a _small troll_ who lived in a _mushroom_ in the city. He had short red _hairy legs_ and a small _spotty face_.

He also had a _sister_ that he called _idiot_ because one of its _eyes_ slightly stuck out, which made his _sister_ _look_ a lot more _stupid_, if that was possible. John had quite a few hobbies. He liked nothing better than to _play bongos,_ read and sometimes _eat snacks_. John loved to _BUY snacks._

But it was on one of these _snack trips_ that he made a _BIG_ _discovery_. John could actually _EAT LOADS_. John thought he was a _greedy troll_. What could he do with this special power? _Nothing_.

He decided he had to _buy all the snacks he could_.

It was _BRILLIANT_.

Good news.

Worksheet's DONE (that was easy) – so I have lots of **free** time now to do some doodles.

Bad news.

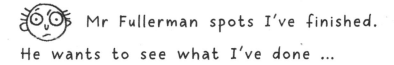 Mr Fullerman spots I've finished. He wants to see what I've done ...

groan.

From the way he's reading my work, I'm guessing it's not going well...

TOM

Interesting answers, but it's clear you didn't read Worksheet One.

Come and see me after the lesson.

Mr Fullerman

THIS is a

BIG PROBLEM.

How am I going to be _first_ 𝕀𝕀𝕀𝕀𝕀𝕀𝕀𝕀 in the queue for my **ULTRAVIOLET** pen **NOW?**

I'll have to **AGREE** with **EVERYTHING** Mr Fullerman says so I can get ~~it~~ away _quickly._
(Yes, Mr Fullerman. Yes, Mr Fullerman.)
Most of my class have probably forgotten all about buying the pens.

It will be fine. I'm [not] worried.

The rest of the day, I'm finding it
hard to concentrate.
Everywhere I L ⊙ ⊙ K there
are kids giving in letters about the
pens or TALKING about buying them.

Yeah!

Now I'm worried I won't get one.
Marcus has already told me FOUR times
that he's buying a pen after school.

> I can't wait to buy a
> pen after school.

(FIVE times. Grrrrrrr.)

When the bell goes for home time, the **WHOLE CLASS** head off in the direction of the **SCHOOL OFFICE!** **EVERYONE** goes apart from ME and Trevor Peters.

I'm **PANICKING NOW!**

I RUSH up to Mr Fullerman's desk while he carries on writing.

"I'll be with you in a minute, boys."

A MINUTE?

That's WAY TOO LONG.

He's still writing. Now he's reading and crossing things off a list.

It's been **l o n g e r** than a minute.

 **"Nearly there."**

He's TAKING AGES. All the pens will have gone by the time I get there.

I ask Trevor if he's going to buy a pen.

He says, "No, I bought one from the shops already."

Phew ... one less person to worry about.

Mr Fullerman is **HUMMING** and drumming his fingers  on the table.

I am desperate to tell him to

 HURRY UP!

But I keep quiet ...

which is NOT easy to do.

AT LAST Mr Fullerman puts down

his pen and says,  "Right, what can I do for you both?"

He doesn't even remember!
I could have snuck out with everyone else.

Trevor reminds him about the worksheets.

"Oh yes ... the worksheets. I need to print off a few more on the photocopier. Come with me, it won't take a minute."

NO, NO, not another minute.

Trevor and I follow Mr Fullerman. I'm trying to walk quickly so he gets the hint that I'm in a BIG  hurry.

Then Mrs WorthingTON STOPS him to have a quick chat.

I want to shout NO STOPPING!
She says, "There's a BIG queue outside the school office, Mr Fullerman."

And I'm thinking, I ⬅ SHOULD BE in that queue!

Then Mr Fullerman wonders if the photocopier is working.

"It might be, but you never know!" Mr Fullerman says, **"Let's go and see, then."**

(YES, LET'S.)

We walk past the queue that goes all the way down the corridor.

I SPOT Derek,

who's near the front. Which is excellent news.

I wave at him and make signs that say...

Pen!

PLEASE GET

ME A **PEN** PLEASE GET

ME A PEN.

I hope he understands.

He knows I've got my pen money with me.

Mr Fullerman loads the photocopier up with paper and says to

"please make sure you read the worksheets in future and DON'T lose them AGAIN."

(I haven't LOST it, I just can't read mine.)

Mush →

I say, "Yes, sir, YES, SIR" in the hope he'll let me go and queue.

The new worksheets are just coming out of the photocopier when the machine suddenly **JAMS.**

Mr Fullerman starts fiddling with the paper and looking to see what's happened.

"This is annoying,"

he says.

(I KNOW!)

To make things worse, kids are coming out of the office holding their pens and torches and waving them around excitedly right under MY NOSE.

Caretaker Stan is busy showing everyone how to use them properly on their bikes.

(Everyone ... apart from ME.)

"Just have to get this paper out,"

Mr Fullerman says...

So I make a | helpful | suggestion.

"We could forget all about the worksheets, sir?"

"No, nearly there. You need them to redo your homework."

Groan...

FINALLY the photocopier starts and
the worksheets

POP out.

HOORAY!

Then Trevor wants to ask a question!

(WHY NOW?)

He wants Mr Fullerman to explain something on the worksheet.

So I tell Mr Fullerman that I understand everything and can I go now?

"No questions then, Tom?"

Only ... WHY did this take SO long?
But I don't say that out loud. Instead I say,
"None, sir,"

and R&VEN...

... to the end of the queue.

There are only a few kids
in front of me. I'm
getting closer to
the front.

Bit closer...

Bit closer.

Nearly there.

When Mrs Mumble starts to shake her head and says, "I'm SO sorry, but we've run out of pens. We'll get some more for next week, I promise. They've been SO popular."

NO NO NO...

This is a disaster.

Mrs Mumble suggests that maybe we could share a pen for now until we get our own?

Good idea.

I go and find Derek.

He's writing on his bike and doing some extra <u>doodles</u>, which is exactly what `I` would be doing

IF I HAD A PEN!!

I tell Derek I missed out on the pens.

"I was too late."

Then I ask if I can use his pen just a tiny bit? And Derek says, "I'm not so sure about that."

Which is <u>not</u> like Derek.

So I say, "I won't use much ... promise."

erek says, "No, it's because..."

"Just a tiny little go?"
And Derek says, "No ... it's because..."
← (Me with a sad face)

Then Derek starts LAUGHING at
me and says, "No, doughnut brain, →
it's because I've bought you one already."

Here.

Derek is a GENIUS.

RESULT!

He does an impression of me:

Without a pen.   With a pen.

I write my name in SPECIAL INVISIBLE INK on my bike. We test out our handiwork with the torches.

It looks AMAZING! GLOWING and very good indeed...

Now I can't WAIT to get home and use it on all my copies of ROCK WEEKLY next (and anything else I can think of).

I know I should really finish my homework and read **WORKSHEET ONE.**

But hey ...

... first things first.

In the morning, I remember something else I have to do. (As well as find another jumper to wear.)

Tell Dad that I've accidentally invited Amy and Florence to the party as well.

"But I have a `plan`..." I say quickly, because Dad's looking at me in a  "what have you done NOW" kind of way. "What's the PLAN then, Tom?"

 "We don't invite the cousins. I can see them another time."

Dad says they have to come or we'll never hear the end of it from Uncle Kevin and Aunty Alice.

"We can't fit everyone in the van now. Uncle Kevin will have to bring the cousins to the party. And I expect he'll want to stay too and make lots of helpful suggestions," he says wearily.

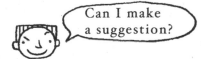

Mum 😊 says she'll mention it to Aunty Alice. Then she tells │me│ that I can't possibly keep wearing such a ridiculously tiny jumper.

(Like it was **MY** fault it shrank in the first place!)

> Throw it in the tumble dryer on ⟨FULL⟩ POWER.

"We'll have to go to the shops to get a new one."

Which is NOT my idea of FUN.

Though I admit it did take me a while to get dressed this morning.

Grrrrrr

SCIENCE

Today my first lesson is SCIENCE.
I can tell it's science because Mr Fullerman
is wearing his **WHITE** COAT.

Occasionally he puts on a pair of
protective goggles
that make his eyes
look even **BIGGER**

than they really are.

I have the most fun in science when we do
experiments.

Mr Fullerman says we are studying:

FORCES in *MOTION.*

(Which sounds sort of interesting, so
I could be in luck.)

I can see there are different experiments
around the classroom. Mr Fullerman puts us in
groups and explains how we have to

**"RECORD YOUR RESULTS IN A
GRAPH AS YOU DO THE EXPERIMENTS".**

Sometimes it's easy to get carried away and
forget. Especially if something odd
happens that you're
not expecting.

wow

Me, Amy, Marcus and Solid are in one group.

The first experiment is timing how long each object takes to fall from a certain height.

(Some objects are more interesting than others.)

Feather

Ball

Book

Paper

Stopwatch
(not for dropping)

100

Marcus has already bagged the stopwatch.
He says it's the "MOST important part of the
experiment".

(Typical.)

The rest of us take turns to drop stuff.

Solid lets the
FEATHER go first.

It takes a while

to land.

N ext Amy does the paper...

But Marcus forgets to press "start".

She has to do it **three** times before he gets it right.

Whoops

I   Sorry

Missed it

(It's not exactly exciting to watch.)

Then it's my turn to drop the book.

Which makes a nice loud

THUD

when it lands.

Marcus still doesn't press the stopwatch in time.

He says, "Do it again."

Solid has to help him. While they're fiddling with the watch, I try one extra experiment with a mint that I have in my bag.

I say to AMY,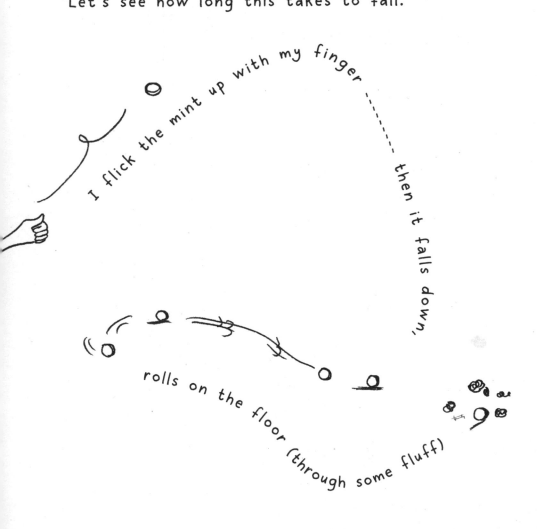
"Let's see how long this takes to fall."

I flick the mint up with my finger ----- then it falls down,

rolls on the floor (through some fluff)

and lands near Mr Fullerman's feet.

I manage to pick it up quickly
before he sees it. Phew!

Marcus has given up on the stopwatch.
He wants to drop the ball instead. Grrrrrr

(We ALL want to get on to the next
experiment now.) come on Marcus

Amy takes over the stopwatch and says,

"OK, GO!"

Marcus doesn't just drop the ball, he

BOUNCES IT REALLY HARD.

The ball hits the

ground, then FLIES back up to the ceiling.

It comes off the ceiling and lands right on Mr Fullerman's head.

Before bouncing a few more times on the ground.

"WHO DID THAT?"

We all keep quiet.

Especially Marcus.

O

Mr Fullerman is looking in OUR ⊙̀ ⊙́ direction and says if it happens again we'll all be in trouble.

Then stupidly I say,
"It was an accident, Mr Fullerman."

Now he thinks I did it!

Marcus just looks at his feet.

Mr Fullerman is in a really **BAD** mood
for the rest of the lesson and keeps his
beady eyes on ME the whole time too.

Marcus says it wasn't his fault.

(It never is.)

(Thanks, Marcus.)

Don't look
at me

Me and Derek are having our lunch.

I'm telling Derek what happened in science when he points to some little kids who are sitting on another table.

He says, "Notice anything odd?"
A lot of the kids in our school are odd, so not really.

The only thing I can see is they all have on what look like ...

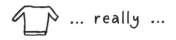 ... really ...

 ... really small ...

 ... jumpers?

I'd forgotten about my jumper.
It feels almost ... normal now.

"Maybe they ALL shrunk in
    the tumble dryer like mine did?"

The kids get up to leave and walk past us.

Derek asks them, "Hey ... why the small jumpers?

"It's a new craze. Even your friend's wearing one too." So I say, "I think you'll find mine is an original SHRINK KNIT."

I lift up my arms (as much as I can) to show them my jumper.

They all look impressed.

Solid is trying not to laugh, which is making him cough.

Derek says, "Now I know how a **NEW** CRAZE gets started..."

And I say, "Yes ... by accident."
I suggest we make eating caramel wafers a new craze?

Derek points out that everyone would start buying them and there would be lot less for us.

Good point. Let's not, then.

$\mathbb{D}$erek and I are walking home when I remember I have (mints🍬) in my pocket!

$\mathbb{I}$ take them out and the first one still has ← fluff on it. I'm just about to flick it off when Marcus *BARGES* in. He says, "Wasn't my fault in science today, you know," and I say, "If you say so, Marcus."

Then he says,
        "Mints ... don't mind if I do."

And just helps himself!

Too late to mention the fluff   now...

 Yum
mint mmmm

He doesn't seem to notice.

I've cheered up and
suggest to Derek that we:

1. Go to Norman's  house for
   BAND practice │ today │
   (see how he is).

2. Buy a few more treats at the shop.
   (Some for 'now,' some for Norman later.)

   TREATS

3. Take treats over to Norman's house
   for band practice.

Derek goes off and we both say

at the same time.

There's SO many things to think about when you're in a band.

MY BIRTHDAY...
(Getting CLOSER)

When I get home, Mum doesn't look too happy because Aunty Alice (who's popped in with the cousins) is telling her all about the wonderful holiday they have planned for this year.

"After a while, one pure white sandy beach starts to look like another," Aunty Alice laughs.

"I'm sure they do," Mum smiles.

Aunty Alice wants to know if we'll be going camping again this year?

And Mum says, "I hope not."

While they carry on
Chit-chatting,

the cousins are searching the

kitchen for snacks.

Mum says, "If you're looking for biscuits, we

don't have any."

But I know someone who does.

So I take the cousins out to see Dad in his

shed.

Dad is mid biscuit bite when we look through the window, which gives him a bit of a shock.

He says he was just having a quick break and best not to mention the secret stash of biscuits to Mum.

Then Dad gives us one each (to keep us quiet, I suspect).

The cousins are looking round the shed, then at me.

Then they ask:

1. Why is my jumper so small? (It's a long story.)

2. What kind of party will I have at **DINO** VILLAGE?

Dad tells them we'll all get to wear special **3D** glasses that make the dinosaurs look **REAL**. The cousins don't look that impressed. Then he adds...

There'll be cake too.

(That works.)

Mmmmm cake

Not long to wait now. We take one more biscuit each and leave Dad to his ~~snacks~~ WORK.

BISCUITS

Back in the house, I'm really hoping that Mum has shown Aunty Alice my birthday wish list. I might have to drop a few hints in case she's forgotten.

Oh look . . . a birthday list

They are both drinking tea and I'm just about to accidentally-on-purpose point to my "birthday list" again when Mum starts

COMPLAINING about...

"**H**orrible **UNWANTED** pests and visitors that come into your garden **AND** sometimes your house and **EAT** absolutely **EVERYTHING!**"

I'm wondering if she means the cousins.

Then Aunty Alice says, "If you're not careful, they **can** grow to be

↑ **ENORMOUS.**"

 (Which is true.)

Those **SLIMY** creatures eat **ALL** my VEGETABLES!

It's only when she mentions | vegetables |

that I realize she means

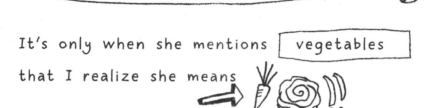

slugs and snails ...

| not | the cousins.

It's an easy mistake to make. (They don't do vegetables.)

Speaking of slimy creatures and unwanted pests...

hile Mum and Aunty Alice are chatting and the cousins watch TV, I'm inspired to do a few drawings.

Cousins peering in the shed

Slime →

Guess who? ←

Slime ↑

Runner bean ↓

More slime

Creature

Mum interrupts my drawing to tell me everything is sorted for my party.

The cousins and Aunty Alice will meet us at **DINO** VILLAGE tomorrow.

It's tricky to keep up with all the stuff that's going on. Which is why I FORGOT about BAND PRACTICE at Norman's house.

Until Derek comes round and reminds me.

(And about changing my jumper too.)

My **DOGZOMBIES** T-shirt
is SO much more comfortable than
my jumper and looks better too.

I've got my guitar and have saved Norman a
few snacks from the shop.

On the way to Norman's,
Derek and I are discussing how Norman
managed to hurt his leg playing CHAMP
with those little kids.

Uh oh

We're impressed that he's managed to stay off school for a

WHOLE WEEK

with just a dodgy leg.

Derek has already called him to say we're coming.

"Norman sounded fine when I spoke to him," he says.

And I say, "Norman will be watching telly with his feet up and **VERY** happy to be missing **MATHS**."

Derek says,

How bad can he be?

... **Much** worse than we thought.

Turns out it wasn't a CHAMP accident after all. Norman ACTUALLY fell off his bike when he got home and badly bruised both his elbows and twisted his ankle.

He tells us, "A twig  blew into my wheel, which made the bike

STOP really suddenly...

I went F L Y I N G through the air...

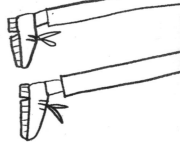
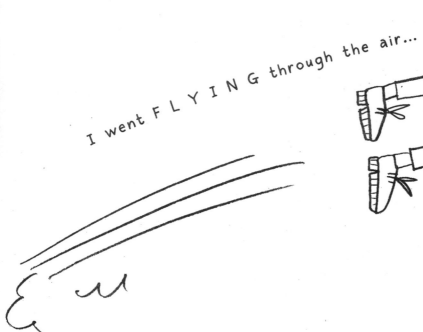

I looked like a SUPERHERO! Right up until I landed..."

weeee

"I'm getting better already," he adds.

Norman says he can STILL play the drums even with his dodgy elbows.

Then he shows us how...

"**I** don't think that's going to work, Norman," Derek says.

I tell Norman we can cancel the school disco gig until he gets better. (He looks a bit disappointed.)

I say, "Besides, we need your **LOUD** drums to drown out mistakes we make."

(Which is true.)

As **DOGZOMBIES** band practice isn't going to happen now, we concentrate on **cheering** Norman up by:

1. Doing an impression of Rooster's EXTRA  fur at the dog show.

Before ...   and after.

2. Doing an impression of Mr Sprocket break-dancing.

Before ...   and after.

Norman is laughing a LOT!

He says we need to stop being funny because it's making his arms hurt.
Which wasn't exactly our plan.

Derek and I leave Norman to "rest". I give him the bag of Snacks I got him.

Derek offers Norman some of his treats too. I guess he's forgotten that...

WILD

Not good if you're trying to recover from sore elbows. Norman seems happy enough, though.

On the way home, Derek and I see more kids wearing small jumpers.

Derek says, "They're everywhere now."

And I say proudly, "It's official, I am a cool trendsetter and not just someone who

didn't want to wear a damp jumper."

Oh yes.

Then Derek reminds me that it's my birthday

TOMORROW!!

Things are just getting better and

BETTER.

(Just like **Norman's**  elbows
and ankle, hopefully.)

YEAH!

A_s SOON as I walk through the
door, Mum wants to know if I have ANY
homework to do.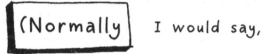

"Get it ALL done before your birthday."

(Normally) I would say,

 "I've got NO homework at all."

But today it's different.)

I SURPRISE Mum  and say,

"I will GET **ALL** my homework

done TONIGHT ON **TIME** ... right **now**."

I'm hoping she is EXTRA impressed.

I take out a calculator to

make Mum think I'm doing difficult maths.

I don't mention the doodling on my

sketchbook. **WORKSHEET ONE** can wait.

This is more fun. AND it's my BIRTHDAY

TOMORROW **TOO**.

(This homework is the best!)

I have FINISHED
my homework EARLY.

(Let me just say that again...)

I have FINISHED
my homework

EARLY and discovered that

my ULTRAVIOLET PEN is even more useful than
I thought. I catch Delia *sneaking* past
my room with THREE copies of

ROCK WEEKLY.

She says they're hers. (They're not.)

Mum hears us arguing and
wants to know

"What's going on?"

I say, "DELIA has been taking MY STUFF."

Then Delia says I am a STUPID BOY who
knows nothing. So I get out my torch
and shine it on one of the
ROCK WEEKLY covers.
And OH YES.

She is SO busted.

TOM'S
ROCK WEEKLY
HANDS OFF DELIA

T hen **M** um says as I've finished my homework early we could "**NIP**" to the shops and pick up a new school jumper.

"And a few other things."

"Like some earplugs," Delia adds helpfully.

Earplugs

Mum gives Delia a 👀 STARE and says, "NO ... things for Tom's birthday."

Delia groans, then *slopes* off back into her room.

I've learnt that when Mum says we'll  _NIP_ somewhere it's supposed to mean it won't take any time at all.

We'll be quick, she says, or "super speedy".

This is NOT TRUE.

 Nip + shopping = AGES and AGES and AGES.

(I still have to go, though.)

Shopping with Mum is a mission.

She keeps choosing really sad **things** for me to try on.

Shame

This is nice

I say, "Mum, I'm <u>not</u> five years old" every time she picks up a pair of trainers that flash when you walk. 😟

   Eventually we find a nice **normal**-size school jumper and a double pack of white T-shirts that are perfect for PE.

T-shirts

I will TRY to remember to bring at least **ONE** of the **T**-shirts to school. That way I can AVOID the

SPARE SPORTS KIT (of shame).

You can <u>EASILY</u> spot the person who's forgotten their PE kit. Everything in the SPARE SPORTS KIT looks a bit ... manky.

Flared tracksuit bottoms!

Then just when I think we've finished
shopping, Mum wants me to try on

THIS HAT.

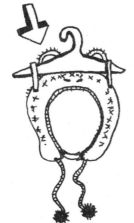

"It's LOVELY ... you used to
have one when you were little."

She says I've been SO good
that for an early birthday treat I can have the
latest copy of **ROCK WEEKLY.**

Then she says...

"Try on the hat first."

(Which is a bit sneaky of her, if you ask me.)

Before I can change my mind, she
SQUEEZES it over my head.

Mum says I look like a sweet little frog and wants to take a photo. That's when I realize the hat has a FACE.

 I am forced to *dive* inside the nearest coat rail and hide.

I tell Mum "I'm not coming out" until she puts her camera away.

And I can't get the stupid hat off because I'm too squashed.

I have to wait until the coast is clear, which takes **AGES** as there are people everywhere. Now I can hear Mum chit-chatting with someone. I don't know WHO she's talking to. No one is seeing me in this stupid hat. I'm staying hidden for as long as I can.

Which is not very long, as the sales assistant suddenly PARTS ALL the coats around me and says,

Oh, hello?

And if that's not bad enough...

Now I can see who Mum's been talking to.

Amy Porter and her mum.

I try and take off the hat, but it gets stuck around my ears and Mum has to help me pull it over my head, like I'm three years old.

Groan.

Amy says, "Nice hat, Tom," and I say,

"Mum made me try it on."

It's all so embarrassing.

I can't leave the shop fast enough.

Mum has to catch up with me and she can see I'm a bit fed up. So she suggests that we go and "get that copy of **ROCK WEEKLY** that I promised you".

Which helps a *bit*.

While we're in the shop, I 👀 spot some **COLOURED ULTRAVIOLET PENS** that can be used on T-shirts. So I tell Mum that if she really wants to cheer me up, these would be good too?

I can see she's { thinking } about it,

so I add,

"I'll spend less time watching telly."

Me
PLEADING

Which does the trick nicely.

(I hope Amy keeps my hat shame to herself.)

It's [not] going to be easy to sleep ⊙ ⊙
tonight because I am

In case anyone forgets about my `birthday`,

I have stuck a few ☐ notes round

the house with some messages on.

TOM's
Birthday
TODAY

YEAH!
My
birthday
today

TOM's
Birthday

Dad comes into my room to say goodnight.

I say, "I can't wait for tomorrow."

And he says, "Why, what's happening tomorrow?
Anything special?"

Like he can't remember.

My dad is hilarious.

I know he's joking because I can hear Mum and Dad wrapping up a present downstairs.

It takes them a while to do ...

it could be a **big** present, then?

Just for a change, I am up REALLY EARLY.

When I run downstairs, I can see someone (Delia) has been busy writing on my notes.

Dad is singing and making pancakes in the kitchen. (They're not pink like the ones Granny Mavis makes.) He says, "Happy birthday, Tom!" But the real surprise is that Delia is holding

Happy Birthday, Tom

something in front of her that looks like a PRESENT [and] a CARD?

Must be a mistake. They can't be for me. On the card it says:

TO MY
IRRITATING LITTLE
BROTHER.

It's for me, then.

Delia being `nice` is a bit odd and must be a STRAIN for her.

She gives me the present and says,

HAPPY BIRTHDAY. Make the most of it.

I open it really carefully in case there's something NASTY inside.

 Mum comes and takes a photo. *smile*

It's only a

DOUBLE PACK OF
CARAMEL WAFERS

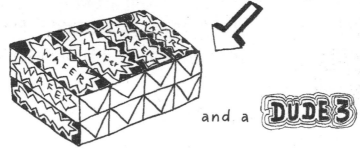

and a

CALENDAR with a with a BIG
pull-out poster!

WOW!

Thanks, Delia. (I'm shocked.) ☺

I'm looking through the calendar and I spot that she has put a gold star on HER birthday. She says,

"I'll be expecting a good present from you on my birthday now."

No pressure, then.

(I can think of a few presents for Delia.)

 **THE FOSSILS** have come round early today and are EXTRA jolly for my

birthday. Granny says

she has bought VERY

SPECIAL home-made

FOOD for the

party.

(I can't look.)

We're here!

Delia's already gone up to her room,
so Granddad thinks he should say (Hello)
and attempt to get
Delia into the *party* mood.

(Good luck with that, Granddad.)

He says, "I'll practise my party entertainment."

Which means he'll be playing the spoons, I think.

WRONG – I forgot about his false-teeth trick. Now Delia is back to being her normal grumpy self again.

I have a really delicious birthday breakfast with Mum and Dad and the Fossils, who occasionally break into song.

Mum and Dad say I can have my present after my PARTY.

Dad says it's a VERY BIG GIFT, so they'll need help bringing it in the house.

(Like it's an elephant or something...)

Granny wants to put "some finishing touches" to her cooking.

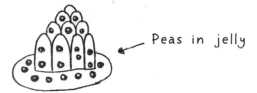

Peas in jelly

This seems like a good time to go to my room and get changed. Best not to watch what Granny does.

Jam

Sausage rolls

My mind gets taken off Granny's

cooking when I hear LOUD
music coming from Delia's room.

I take a ⊙ ⊙ look through the crack
in the door and see Delia

DANCING
(well, sort of head-banging) to a rock track.

Her sunglasses KEEP falling
off when she shakes her head.

It's hilarious.

Then I watch while she sticks them back on to her head with a bit of tape!

I'm trying not to laugh.

But I can't help it.

Delia spots me and tells me to

GET LOST.

I say, "Be nice to me, it's my birthday."

She says, **"GET LOST,** please."

(Very funny.)

And make sure you keep your stinky friends **out** of my room when I'm not here."

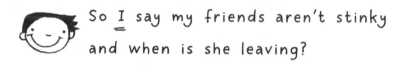 So I say my friends aren't stinky and when is she leaving?

And she says, "Right now."

I think Delia's forgotten about the sticky tape on her head.

sticky
TAPE

As she's on the way out of the house, I *could* remind her.

Because she does look a bit stupid.

...But why bother?

As I have some spare time before everyone arrives for the party, I decide to put it to good use and try out my **COLOURED ULTRAVIOLET PENS** on my new WHITE T-shirts.

I have LOTS of good ideas for BOTH of them.

It will be a SUPER secret design that I can wear in school. No one will see it unless they have a special torch, which is not likely to happen in PE.

This one could be a good birthday present for Delia, I think? (When they DRY you won't be able to see ANYTHING.)

How kind

Suits you

I've just finished my T-shirts when Derek arrives.

Happy BIRTHDAY, Tom!

Then Mark Clump and Solid turn up next with what look like very interesting presents.

Mum says I'm not allowed to open them until we get back from **DINO** VILLAGE.

Amy arrives next ... without Florence?

She says, "Florence is sick and can't come."

And I say that's a shame and it's usually Julia Morton who gets sick (as a joke).

And Amy says, "Funny you should mention Julia."

Because Amy forgot that Julia was coming to HER house today.

She says, "Would it be OK if Julia came instead of Florence?"

And I say "Sure," which is just as well, as Julia is already here.

Hello, Tom

Granny is offering some of her special fish biscuits around and some EXTRA-crunchy finger biscuits to Julia.

Granny says, "Don't worry, they're not real fingers!"

(But Julia is already looking a bit pale.)

Then Granny wonders if "anyone would like to try a cheese and chocolate sandwich?"

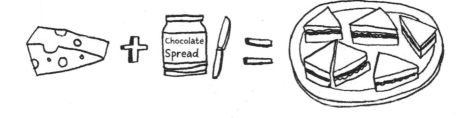

Maybe later, Granny.

(Much later.)

Mum is staying at home with **THE FOSSILS** to get everything ready for when we get back from the party.

Dad is in the van and ready to go.

He's **hooting** and **ROARING** the engine outside.

Everyone thinks Dad hired the **DINO** VAN especially for the party.

(WOW!)

I don't tell them we go to the supermarket in it too.

Mum has sent us off with a few CARAMEL WAFERS  for the journey.

YEAH!

They keep us going until we arrive.

Uncle Kevin and the cousins are already waiting outside. He thinks that Dad has gone to a lot of trouble hiring a special van for the party.

"That must have cost a bit?" Uncle Kevin asks.

Dad says, "It was a bit pricey, but money well spent."

(I'm sure he told Mum the van was free?)

I got the
van for
FREE!

But I don't say anything because I've just

seen the **DINO** VILLAGE...

... entrance.

It's AMAZING!

3D DINO VILLAGE
ENTRANCE

Inside we meet Larry,  our **DINO** GUIDE.

He's very dramatic and $LOUD.$ He says, "Are you ready to go on a journey into the unknown where dinosaurs will come to $LIFE?$"

We all say  apart from Julia,

who says, "Sort of."

Amy whispers,

"Your granny's finger biscuits creeped her out a bit." Which I can understand.

Uncle Kevin asks Dad what he's been up to lately and Dad says, "This and that," just when someone calls out Dad's name. *"Hello, Frank! Is this your son, then?"*

(He's pointing to me.)

Dad int oduces us to Mr Rex, who is the manag r of **DINO** VILLAGE.

Dad explains to Uncle Kevin that he's been redesigning a lot of the posters and promotional material for **DINO** VILLAGE.

Dad asks Mr Rex, "I hope it's bringing in some new customers?"

And Mr Rex says,

"It's the promotional VAN we lent you that people are seeing **everywhere**. *Even the supermarket! So that's doing its job – keep up the good work!"*

Dad is smiling in a slightly embarrassed way.

He says it's all part of a big marketing plan.
(Whatever that means.)

Larry is busy handing out the

 glasses we have to wear on

the **DINO** VILLAGE TRAIN.

Dad says that compared to a normal theme
park, **DINO** VILLAGE is quite "compact".

(He means small.)

We still have to get on a mini train that takes us on the **3D DINO** STORY TOUR (it's a bit like a ghost train at a fairground).

So far ... IT'S AMAZING!

We travel through all sorts of different scenes. There's loads to look at.

The cousins are already laughing at all the

SCARY stuff that's supposed to

make you J U M P.

There are plenty of sound effects too.

Derek keeps shouting in my ear every time a

dinosaur roars.

The whole tour is fantastic.

The last scene is the pretend village.

Larry tells us to "look out for the

DINOSAURS that have escaped into the village."

The train slows right down.

A **MASSIVE ROAR**

makes the train shake. It's quite scary.
(This is what I see.)
↓

The roar gets louder. And with our

 3D glasses on it feels

like we're being chased by a HUGE

DINOSAUR.

The train takes  *OFF*
JUST in time for us to get away safely.

Solid says, **How brilliant was that?**

Everyone agrees. Apart from Julia, who still looks a little pale.

Uncle Kevin thinks it was

very well done and jokes that "Frank had a full head of hair when he arrived".

Larry shows us around the rest of the "village", which includes a REPTILE and creature **section**.

Larry says we can take turns in holding a very hairy 5Pider.

"Who'd like to go first?"

Julia doesn't seem keen.

Mark Clump is, and so are the cousins, who volunteer first.

Uncle Kevin says they are

"very brave boys and not SCARED of anything".

"They take after me," he adds.

 Then Larry tells Uncle Kevin,

"It's your turn next" and puts the spider on his arm before he can change his mind.

"Hold still, I'll take a photo of all you brave boys together," Dad says.

Suddenly Uncle Kevin doesn't look quite so brave.

When the spider's removed, he breathes a HUGE sigh of relief.

Larry tells us our table is ready in THE **DINO** VILLAGE CAFE. And we all cheer.✻

YEAH!

Everyone is STARVING.

Apart from Julia, who's not hungry at all.

Gulp

My special table does look a *bit* like a little kid's party ... but I don't care.

We can still hear loud **ROARING** in the background.

Which makes us all jump when we're least expecting it. Dad says it sounds like my stomach rumbling. (True.)

On the menu we have a choice of:

Wriggly worms with tomato sauce (spaghetti, of course).

Juicy **DINO** burger and jungle salad (beef burger and normal salad).

Fresh **DINO** BIRD in breadcrumbs (chicken). And lots and lots of other weird things.

I say to Derek, "It's like something Granny Mavis would cook."

While I'm reading the menu, I realize something ⊙ ⊙ looks **VERY** familiar. I can't think what it is, though. The posters are reminding me ... what is it?

I'm trying to remember. When the **BIG** jug of **DINO SLIME** arrives I get distracted (it's apple juice, I think). It even has ICE CUBES with creatures frozen inside them.

"Not real ones, of course," I tell Julia.

My party is going very well.

Amy and Julia seem to be enjoying themselves.

Solid has a sore throat from

SHOUTING too much. He says the
DINO SLIME is making him feel better.

Dad takes pictures of us
and everyone together.

Then Mark Clump gives me a
small box. He says, "Don't open it now" as
it's only part of my present. The rest of it is
back at my house.

But I haven't opened ANYTHING yet,
so I say thanks and decide to take just a
sneaky peek inside to see what it is...

Which is a bit of a mistake.

Because out pop THREE little
GRASSHOPPERS.

They jump down the table and I try
and catch them before they escape!
Bits of food are flying everywhere as Solid
keeps grabbing the plates.

The grasshoppers

LEAP

on to **U**ncle Kevin and he goes

CRAZY.
He's brushing himself
down, saying, "Get them off me. Get them off
me." While Dad is busy taking more photos.

SMILE

Mark Clump manages to catch two and Derek
gets the last one.

I pop them back in the box and say
"Whoops" to Mark, who says,

I did
warn you!

Point taken.

Dad keeps taking pictures of the party when the lights suddenly go down and someone comes in holding a BIG dinosaur cake with candles.

Everyone sings HAPPY BIRTHDAY and I blow them all out.

When the lights go up, I notice that the waiter is wearing a VERY SILLY COSTUME. It's a spotty dinosaur outfit with glittery boots. I'm sure I've seen that costume somewhere before?

I double-check it's not Dad in the costume.
(It's not ... phew!)

And **THAT'S** when I remember: I saw the costume in our

HOUSE!

I nudge Derek and tell him where I've seen that costume before and how I thought my dad was going to wear it to the school disco!

"Imagine if my dad had come to our school disco wearing that stupid costume. How embarrassing would that have been?"

Derek says, "Shame."

We eat some cake and check out the DINO GOODY BAGS for more treats. It's been a really fun party.

— DINO teeth!

Dad takes a few more photos of us on the way out.

Now I'm telling **A**my and Julia about the costume, and how I'd PANICKED because I thought Dad was going to be the DJ at the school disco wearing THAT costume. They both laugh.

Ha! Ha! Ha! Ha!

"Can you imagine the SHAME of
ALL those kids looking at my dad in that
dinosaur costume?"

Then Amy says, "Tom, I think you should
come and see this."

Amy says, "Isn't THAT your dad?" and
I say, "Yes ... that is my dad, in the
dinosaur costume with the glittering
boots on and everything."

Oh great.

In the van going home I keep seeing

THAT poster

EVERYWHERE!

Mark Clump and Solid

are playing Spot the

DINO Poster.

So far Dad's been on the

side of a BUS.

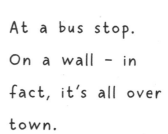

There's
another

At a bus stop.
On a wall – in
fact, it's all over
town.

Dad says it was part

of the job he did for

DINO VILLAGE.

"Besides, it was easier and cheaper to be in the poster myself. Why wouldn't I do it?"

And I say,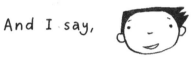

"NOT to embarrass me on my birthday or any other day of the week?"

Seems like a good reason to me?

Everyone says it's not **THAT** bad and you can't tell it's my dad in the poster.

Which is not true. But I will just have to get used to them being ...

EVERYWHERE!

When we get home, Granny Mavis has put out some of her home-made treats, which are interesting.

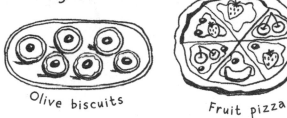

Olive biscuits   Fruit pizza

At least I get to open my

PRESENTS now.

It takes my mind off the POSTERS. Derek has bought me...

OH YES! **DUDE 3**'s

NEW CD.   EXCELLENT!

 He says he might have to borrow it too. Which is fine by me.

Solid has got me some EXCELLENT ROCK T-shirts and a MASSIVE

packet of caramel wafers.

(A perfect combination.)

Amy's present is some VERY nice drawing pens that change colour when you mix them and a drawing book too.

"I know you like doodling," she says. "And don't forget this one."

ANOTHER present!

I open it up and Mum says, "How lovely! Amy remembered!"

So she did...
"It suited you, Tom. I thought you'd want to wear it for the next **DOGZOMBIES** gig!"
Amy is joking. (I hope.)

Mum and Granny say "Awwwww" really loudly and want me to try it on.

That's not going to happen.

I change the subject and open the card Julia has brought me...

It has MONEY inside.   YEAH!

Then Mark gives me the rest of his present.

He says, "You don't have to keep the grasshoppers. They were a clue to what the real present is. I can give them to my snake."

I'm wondering what my real present is now?

I t's part two of:

 The cousins tell me, "It's a really good film, not SCARY at all." I say, "I'll definitely watch it."

VAMPIRE SWAMP
MONSTERS vs
SWARMING
BLOODSUCKING
GRASSHOPPERS

(I don't say ... from behind a cushion, which is how I usually watch scary films.)

 Then the cousins give me their present.

It's a mini sea creature kit.

I've ALWAYS wanted one of those!

SEA creatures are really tiny and

HATCH out when you put them in

water and feed them

special food.

The pictures on the side show

the creatures living in

their own

homes.

I ask the cousins if they really look like that. And they say, "No ... they look really weird."

 Which should be interesting to see.

T ime to open my  PRESENT from Mum and Dad.

T hey look more excited than me.

 Hurry up! (Especially Dad.)

I open it up and it's ... a GUITAR SONGBOOK?

I give it a SHAKE in case there's any money in it.

You never know.

No, nothing.

Oh well, I need a guitar songbook, so that's good. :)

I'm flicking through it and showing it to Derek when Mum tells me to go into the kitchen.

"Can you get me a tissue, please, Tom?"
And I'm wondering why I have to go? It is my birthday, after all.

T hen Dad says...

"Hurry up, Tom." I roll my eyes at Derek and say, "Won't be long," then go into the kitchen.

And there's a ...

GUITAR SHAPED PRESENT

FOR ME!!

From Mum and Dad and the Fossils!

Oh YES

Derek is almost as excited as me. He says it's a shame we're not playing the DOGZOMBIES gig at the school disco now, so I can use my guitar. (It's not.)

WOW

Me being pleased

I'm so happy I actually HUG Mum and Dad and the Fossils in front of all my friends.

Whooo hoooo!

Just before everyone goes home, Granddad decides to entertain us by playing the SPOONS. It goes down surprisingly well until Granny starts singing along. Which is a bit embarrassing for my friends (and me).

Then Grandad juggles with three sausages while Dad takes a photo.

He is so busy smiling for the camera ...

... he accidentally drops one sausage in the jug of orange juice.

Mum has made me another cake (or a {proper} cake, as she tells Aunty Alice).

It's a ... **DOGZOMBIES** CAKE. WOW!

While Mum's busy cutting the cake, Delia slopes in. She's been avoiding me and my friends today. **THE FOSSILS** are making everyone laugh and Dad's still taking photos while Delia helps herself to a drink.

She's too busy being grumpy to notice anything odd dropping into her glass.

I'm <u>not</u> going to tell her about the sausage in the juice. She can find that out for herself...

I've had a **BRILLIANT** birthday party.

I say  and thanks

to everyone again as they leave. Uncle Kevin wants to know how Dad's photos have turned out.

Dad says, "Really well ... especially the ones with you and the grasshoppers. I'll send copies."

Mum thinks I should get ready for bed.

But it's FAR too early
and I'm not sleepy at ALL. ⊙ ⊙

I go to my room and listen
to DUDE 3's new album, which is

FANTASTIC.

I have to keep turning the music down so Mum
thinks I'm going to bed. Instead I do some
drawing with my new pens in my new book.

PENS   My DOGZOMBIES birthday
cake has reminded me that due
to Norman's elbows, we're
NOT playing at the school disco.

At least we have a **REAL** excuse not to play this time.

   I had thought of a few more excuses if we needed them (just in case).
Like:
• My guitar was abducted by aliens.

BYE

   • Derek's keyboard shrank
      in the rain.

   • A monster ate
      Norman's drum kit.

Yum!

Not sure how well they would have worked? I can use them another time.
(I'll just swap guitar/keyboard/drum kit for HOMEWORK.)

Now Dad pops his head round the door
and says, "Hey, birthday boy ...
bed now."

But I'm desperate to listen to **DUDE 3**
just one more time. I put on my headphones
and because **DUDE 3** are SO good, I
start singing ... just a little bit.

Delia BANGS on my door and
she says, "What's that Horrible noise?
SHUT UP, will you?"

So I say, "It's still my birthday ... be nice."

Then she says,  "SHUT UP, will you ... please."

I ignore her and carry on singing, only

MUCH LOUDER this time.

Then Delia tells me that if I promise

to stop singing she'll buy me

another present.

Stupidly, I say,

Really?

And she says, "Yes, singing lessons. You sound like a freak. Shut up or I'll take back the calendar I gave you."

I've had such a good birthday that not even Delia can spoil it now. The rest of the weekend she keeps trying, though.

I manage to ignore her and RELAX. There's a bit of leftover cake to eat and I even try Granny's finger biscuits.

Mum is busy looking at all the photos Dad took. She's laughing at the ones of Uncle Kevin.

Dad says we mustn't forget to send him copies.

"**A**re you sure he'll want them?" Mum says.

Then Dad says, "Oh yes. This one's my particular favourite." (Who knew grasshoppers could be so scary?)

Check this out

Excellent

I 've brought a couple of the best photos in to show everyone who was at the party. Amy says she had a really good time (which is nice).

 Then Marcus BUTTS in and says, "It must have been SO embarrassing for you."

I say, "Not really, my Uncle Kevin was quite funny." ☺

And he says, "No, I mean YOUR DAD wearing that dinosaur costume on ALL those posters EVERYWHERE?"

I'd forgotten about the POSTER.

Thanks for reminding me, Marcus.
So I say, "It's not *that* bad.
Besides, hardly anyone knows
it's │ my │ dad."

Marcus says, "They might now."
    Great. Trust him to **BLAB** about that
POSTER.

    Oh well, I'm not going to let him spoil the
rest of my day.

Because Mr Fullerman says we have

"something important to do right NOW."

(We do? Not more TIMES-TABLE SQUARES, please.)

Then he asks me to come to the **FRONT**
of the class. I'm trying to think of anything
I've done wrong?

Normal-sized
jumper?

On time today?

Homework?
Maybe/maybe not.

Then Mr Fullerman and the whole class suddenly
start singing ...

HAPPY BIRTHDAY

to me.

Marcus is singing and doing an L-shaped sign on his head at the same time (for "loser"), which is nice of him.

It's a bit embarrassing, but I say thanks to everyone and take a bow. Then I remember to say that sadly, due to Norman's dodgy elbows, DOGZOMBIES won't be playing at the school disco this year. But add that Norman is really looking forward to coming back to school.

(He's not; I made that bit up. But it sounds good.)

From the look on Mr Fullerman's face, I think he's forgotten we had to cancel.

He says, **"Mr Keen will be very disappointed ... again."**

(I could give him a few excuses for Mr Keen if he needs them?)

Aliens took Dogzombies away

I see

"Let's hope the DJ is as good as your band, Tom," Mr Fullerman adds.

I hope the **DJ** is:

1. Better than **DOGZOMBIES**.

2. NOT my dad.

3. NOT Derek's dad.

Mr Fullerman hands back our
sketchbooks and inside there is some
MORE

for me!

Really <u>excellent</u> sketchbook cover, Tom.

6 Merits

I will ask Mr Keen to mention your good work in next month's newsletter.

Mr Fullerman

Mr Fullerman is possibly my
FAVOURITE teacher EVER.

I have SIX MERITS for my sketchbook cover AND I'm going to be in the next **NEWSLETTER** too!

 (I WILL show it to Mum and Dad this time.)

This worksheet was stuck in my sketchbook too.

The Natural World

Look closely at various plants, trees, flowers, fruit, landscapes and anything from the natural world. Then, using your pencils and pens, draw as many different objects as you can that show:

Different textures
Curved shapes
Hard edges
Light and shade
Straight lines
Round shapes

Keep drawing everything you see around you and make notes of the date you did the drawing.

Marcus is LOOMING over my shoulder trying to look at my sketchbook.

So I start drawing something...

He's still looking. ⊙ ⊙

He wants to know what I'm drawing.

The Natural World

Look closely at various plants, trees, flowers, fruit, landscapes and anything from the natural world. Then, using your pencils and pens, draw as many different objects as you can that show:

Different textures
Curved shapes
Hard edges
Light and shade
Straight lines
Round shapes

Keep drawing everything you see around you and make notes of the date you did the drawing.

So I say...   Guess?

I think Marcus has just realized what I've been drawing.

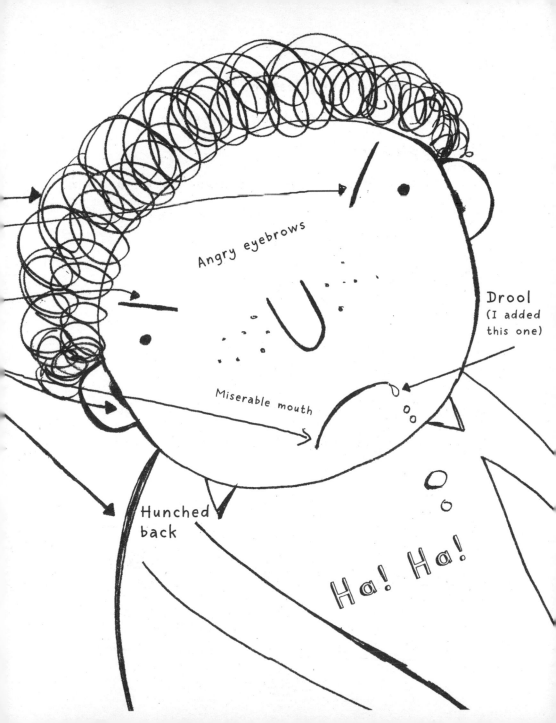

Angry eyebrows

Drool
(I added
this one)

Miserable mouth

Hunched
back

Ha! Ha!

At the end of the lesson, Mr Fullerman suggests that we should make Norman a GET WELL SOON card.

Which is a good idea. He gives us all a plain white sticker to draw and sign our names on.

I do a monster eating a biscuit. Because Norman likes monsters and biscuits. Amy draws a smiling cat to cheer Norman up. And Marcus draws a worm ...

why?

He says, "It's a GET WELL SOON WORM."

Of course it is, silly me.

Then everyone puts the stickers on a giant card.

I'm sure Norman will really like it.

He won't be quite as keen on the mountain of schoolwork Mr Fullerman is sending home for him to catch up on.

FOR NORMAN WATSON
5F

Posters for the school *disco* are up EVERYWHERE now.

Some people are getting VERY excited.

 There are kids practising
their dances at lunchtime
too.

Derek suggests we could
join in and show them some of our
ROCK STAR poses?

And I say, "We <u>could</u> ... OR we could keep our excellent reputation and **NOT** look stupid?"

Because I can ⊙ ⊙ see Amy, Florence, Indrani and Julia are all sitting on a bench within WATCHING distance. Instead Derek starts to wonder which teachers will do the MOST embarrassing dancing this year.

And I say, "ALL OF THEM."

Derek does a WOBBLE DANCE and tells me,

"This is Mr Keen." Which
is really funny.

I do a mad POGO dance, jumping up
and down.

"Who's this?"

"Mrs Mumble?"

"NO."

"Mr Fullerman?"

"YES!"

Then I do another one. A REALLY silly
dance, *swaying* from side *to side*.

"Who's this then, Derek?"

He's not answering.

"**G**uess who? You know ... Mrs..."

I'm swaying and making swirly moustache moves
with my hands.
I give him another hint
by pointing to my top lip.

Then Derek says...

"Tom ... Mrs Worthington ...

Mrs Worthington!"

And I say, "YES! I bet she dances JUST like that!"

"*You'll just have to wait and see, Tom,*" Mrs Worthington tells me.

How was I supposed to know she was standing right behind me?

I can hear ALL the girls laughing in the background too.

(That's just great, then.)

Marcus says he saw me dancing
"like an idiot at lunchtime".

And I say, "I was pretending to dance
like Mrs Worthington."
(I admit, it was embarrassing.)

Marcus starts telling me what a good
dancer HE is and how EVERYONE will be
watching ☉ ☉ HIM at the
school disco.

"I'll be wearing my specially

signed DUDE3 T-shirt too."
Mr Fullerman comes to my rescue. He tells
Marcus to **"stop talking in class"**.

(Thanks, Mr Fullerman...) I haven't even THOUGHT about what I'll be wearing to the disco. I'll probably just wear whatever's nearest. Or I might wear my T-shirt?

That'll do

Later that afternoon, Mrs Mumble makes an announcement over the TANNOY. She says:

ANY sTUdents wearing Very small jumpers Please make Sure you have the Correct Size tomorrow. Thank you.

Not me, then.

$\mathcal{J}$ust in case we didn't get the message, we get a letter to take home too.

From: Oakfield School

Dear Parents and Carers,

It has come to my attention that many of the children seem to be wearing very small jumpers to school.

These uniform changes seem to creep in from time to time.

Please can I ask everyone to ensure they have the correct size jumper in future.

Yours sincerely,
Mr Keen
Headmaster

That's my SHRINK KNIT craze over with. It was fun while it lasted.

SCHOOL DISCO!

I make sure I put the **RIGHT** school jumper on this morning, as Mr Keen will be checking EVERYONE at the school gates and probably the school disco too.

small

BIG

Huh.

If you've got a small jumper on you're not coming in...

Today, I have my **least** favourite subjects **ALL** day long.

SOMEHOW I *FORCE* myself to stay WIDE AWAKE and perky right through...

Maths (first).

Followed by spelling (which was TOUGH).

T hen history (no programmes to watch, either).

I survived.

It's AMAZING.

M y last lesson today is with
Mr Fullerman and he asks us to
design a BIG poster. He says...
**"Imagine you're attracting new pupils
to come to OAKFIELD SCHOOL. Tell
me what is special about the school.
Explain why you like your teachers.
What is the BEST thing about this
school?"**

I say very quietly to Amy, "Small poster, then."

Forgetting about Mr Fullerman's

SUPERHUMAN hearing.

He gives me a **"get on with your work"** stare. I wait until his back is turned to do a few doodles. Nothing fancy.

Then he tells me to...

"STOP DOODLING

AND START WRITING."

Mr Fullerman hasn't even turned round!
How does he do that?

Marcus keeps nudging me and saying he knows ALL the words to DUDE3's new songs and he has some good dance moves too.

So I say, "Good for you, Marcus."

He's being extra annoying today.

I have a few ideas for the poster now.

COME TO OAKFIELD SCHOOL

IF you like:

★ ANNOYING KIDS.

★ WATCHING TEACHERS DANCE IN VERY WEIRD WAYS.

★ TEACHERS who have SUPERHUMAN POWERS ⊙ ⊙ X-RAY EYES that see everything you do.

★ SUPERSONIC EARS that hear everything you say.

★ Wearing spare **MANKY** PE kit.

Never a dull moment

at OAKFIELD SCHOOL.

TRUE

Good poster. I think that says it all.

I wasn't that bothered about the school disco until I saw some of the good SNACKS we'll be able to get tonight.

Suddenly I am EXTRA KEEN to go.

When I get home, Delia is in her room listening to MY NEW **DUDE 3** album.

I tell her to hand it over **NOW**. She says it's hers and she has bought her own copy.

It's mine

I need my SPECIAL torch to check for my SECRET mark. But I can't find it anywhere.

It's **disappeared**.

Ha!
Ha!

My CD →

MY torch

Boots

Which is really annoying.

From the way Delia is laughing I bet she knows where it is ... grrrrr.

I decide to deal with my grumpy sister later as Derek will be round soon and I have to get ready for the **SCHOOL DISCO**.

Not that putting on a T-shirt will take that long. But there's a small problem... I'm not totally sure which T-shirt is the GRUMPY DELIA T-shirt and which is the COOL one I made?

When Derek turns up, he can't tell either.

"Wear this one," he says.

I'm going to bring the other one too, just in case he's wrong.

Good thinking.

Dad offers to give us a lift back to school so we're not late for the ~~snacks~~ disco.

When Dad pulls up outside, LOADS of people are staring at us.

I keep forgetting about the **DINO** VAN.

Derek and I go inside where the school hall is
all done up like a proper
disco, with lights
flashing everywhere.

We're busy looking for the snacks when some
kids come up and ask,
"Is that your dad on all those posters around
town dressed as a dinosaur?"

Great, that's all I need.
So I say the only thing I can in this
situation...

"**No**, that's NOT my dad. Why would you even think that?"

The kids point to Marcus, who is standing at the back of the hall.

"That boy there's been telling EVERYBODY it's your dad."

Groan...

Thanks, Marcus.

I'm NOT going to let him ruin my evening. I suggest Derek and I should go and get some juice. Which is a good idea.

"H_{ey}, I can see the drawing on your T-shirt now," Derek says.

He's right.

"Must be **ULTRAVIOLET** light like the torches."

My eyes are glowing too.

At least I'm wearing the right one.

Which does look amazing.

Then Mr Keen announces that we have a VERY special DJ tonight.

"Give a BIG Oakfield welcome to…"

Mr SPROCKET

He says, "YO, everyone."

Which is embarrassing.

A bit like his outfit.

He puts on some LOUD music that brings a few more people on to the dance floor.

Boys are whizzing round and skidding on their knees while other kids do a **ROBOT** dance in a line.

Most of the girls stick together on the other side of the hall, chatting and laughing.

The teachers try to encourage everyone to join in.

Mrs Worthington is dancing EXACTLY like I thought she would.

Mr Fullerman is giving some of the boys one of his STARES, which stops them from skidding too much.

Careful boys

When Mr Sprocket only goes and puts on a DUDE3 SONG, Derek and I rush to do some air punching and pretend guitar playing (which we are very good at).

Marcus is jumping up and down near us. He's got his eyes closed and is SPINNING around and BUMPING into EVERYONE.

He says, "OUT OF MY WAY!" which is annoying.

Then he BUMPS into me.

So I BUMP into HIM.

Which makes him BUMP RIGHT BACK into me (on purpose).

But I manage to ═══ *swerve* out of his way and he goes *FLYING* across the dance floor and

CRASHES

right into Mrs Mumble.

Whoops

DUDES

Who's holding a MASSIVE plastic jug of water for Mr Sprocket.

Well, not any more. Marcus is soaking wet and starts pointing at ME saying I *pushed* him. Like it's MY FAULT!

Mrs Mumble thinks we should BOTH be more careful.

Caretaker Stan is busy cleaning up the floor
so there are no more accidents.
Mrs Mumble thinks Marcus might have to go
home early.

 "Unless you borrow
something DRY to wear
from the spare kit box?"

Then Derek reminds me that I have a SPARE
T-shirt that Marcus can borrow.

 And I say, "Oh yes, so I do."

Mrs Mumble thinks that's a good idea.
So I go and give it to Marcus, who doesn't
even say thank you.

Derek tells Marcus not to stand to near the **ULTRAVIOLET** light with the T-shirt on.

And Marcus says, "Whatever."

(So it's not like we didn't warn him.)

Mr Sprocket has been playing lots of good music (surprisingly). He's trying hard not to start dancing himself.

It's nearly the end of the disco when Mr Sprocket says...

"Is everyone ready to JUMP?"

We are.

There's a big crowd of kids all gathering around in a circle.

"Everybody JUMP JUMP!"

Me and Derek jump over to join in.

Amy, Florence and Indrani are there too. There's a very big crowd who seem to be watching someone in the middle of the group dancing.

I don't think it's one of the teachers.

And it's not Norman (as he still has dodgy elbows).

D erek and I jump up to see who it is.

It looks like Marcus, who's jumping ^{up} and down.

"He's enjoying all the attention he's getting," I say to Derek.

When the song's over, he comes over to us and is looking EXTRA smug.

He says, "I told you everyone would be watching ME because I am SUCH a good dancer."

And I say, "Yes, Marcus, that's
exactly why everyone was
looking at you..."

I tell Marcus he can keep the T-shirt because it really suits him.

Derek and I agree that this year's school disco has been...

EXCELLENT.

☺

I enjoyed jumping and dancing a lot more than I expected to.

Mr Fingle, Derek's dad, picks us up. He says, "It's **SUCH** a shame I couldn't DJ this year."

(It's not.)

Derek says that Mr Sprocket did a good job and will probably do it again next year and the following year too.

(He's making sure his dad NEVER DJs again, I think.)

When I get home I'm going to have a quick play on my

NEW GUITAR.

(YEAH!)

I am in a REALLY good mood ...

... until I walk though the door and hear

music coming from MY room.

It's DELIA again, messing with my stuff.
I HAVE to tell Mum and Dad what
she's up to. But I can't find them
in the kitchen ...
... in the front room or upstairs.
Delia's not in her room either.
Because she's in MINE.
So I open the door to catch her and say,

GET out of
my room and
leave my
stuff alone.

And Mum says:

"Hi, Tom ... did you have a good time?"

Now I'm wondering why EVERYONE is in my

room?

Dad says he's learnt to play a new DUDE 3

song on the guitar. And I have to remind him

that it's <u>MY</u> GUITAR in case he's forgotten.

He's actually not bad.

Even Delia's impressed.

Dad says it's easy to learn.

I say, "If I had my guitar back?"

I take the opportunity of Mum and Dad being in my room to tell Delia I want my special torch back too. "I know you have it."

Mum suggests she goes and gets it.

Which is good.

Then Mum says that we are such a musical family we should all be in a band together...
"Like the Partridge family."

I have no idea what she's talking about, but it sounds like a terrible idea.

Dad eventually gives me my guitar back.

And I manage to work out a bit of the **DUDE 3** song as well.

DOGZOMBIES should learn to play this too.

We might finally get to play in front of the whole school, which would keep Mr Keen happy.

It could be

AMAZING...

... Well, sort of.

ants

more...

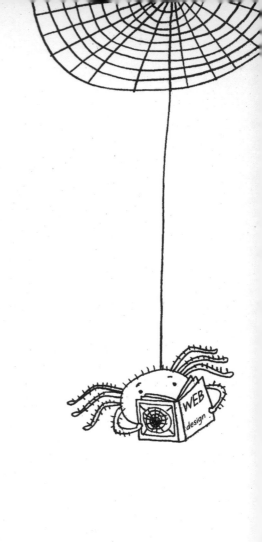

ha ha!

How to make TOAST DOODLES
(from page 3)

Nice **fresh bread**

Clean **hands**

Take a slice of bread.

Press the bread down.

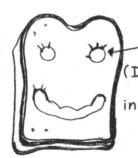

Like this.
(Dents pressed into the bread.)

Then TOAST bread. (Be careful and get an adult to help!)

The TOAST goes brown but stays white where you've pressed down. Ta da! Yum.

Have You Got ALL the TOM GATES books yet?

ALL NEW COVERS!

www.scholastic.co.uk/tomgatesworld